CYNTHIA HICKEY

THE LIBRARIAN'S LAST CHAPTER

CYNTHIA HICKEY

Copyright © 2014 Cynthia Hickey

This book is a work of fiction. Names, characters, places, and incidents are the product of the author's imagination and are used fictitiously. Any resemblance to actual events, locales, or persons, living or dead, is coincidental.

No part of this book may be copied or distributed without the author's consent.

All rights reserved.

ISBN-13: 978-1-0880-6126-8

To God for yet another fun book to write,

To my husband for his never-ending encouragement,

And to my agent for the opportunity to continue writing mysteries.

Thank you all!

1

"Don't be so dramatic, Marsha Calloway Steele. It's not like you're facing a firing squad."

It might as well be. Volunteering in the high school library isn't my idea of a good time. How did I let my best friend, Lynn Marshall, talk me into such a thing? Wasn't the PTO or Parent Teacher Organization enough torture?

I scooted farther against my bed pillows, cradling the cordless phone to my ear. "Couldn't I do something behind the scenes where I didn't have to deal with other parents?"

Lynn laughed. "The librarian wants to do a big book donation rally with a book fair, snacks, everything. It's a really big deal, and she needs your help. I volunteered you, not thinking it would be such a big inconvenience. You're nothing but a big scaredy-cat."

"Yep, and proud of it." I grabbed several dark-chocolate M&Ms and popped them in my mouth. "You know I don't have a lot of time to volunteer. Not with the store." Being a co-owner of Country

Gifts from Heaven kept me very busy. That and the occasional dead body I tended to stumble across every few months. I'd resigned myself to accepting the gift of finding trouble.

"Besides, Mrs. Grimes is very, um, not nice."

"You can manage for a week or two. We need you. Bye." She hung up on me.

Mrs. Grimes still had the same way of looking over her glasses and staring a person into submission as she had when I was in high school. The woman scared me, plain and simple, and now my best friend wanted me to work with the woman for two weeks?

I should never have filled out the volunteer paperwork and been fingerprinted. All it brought me was more work.

I crawled from bed and into the shower. If I was going to work at the library, there was no time to start like the present. Mom wouldn't mind holding down the fort at the store for an hour or two while I found out exactly what Mrs. Grimes had in store for me.

The hot water helped to wash away some of the apprehension, and by the time I had my hair fixed and a five-minute makeup job done, I felt confident I could handle one old librarian well past retirement age.

Grabbing my purse off the foyer table, I headed to my blue Prius. After getting the okay from Mom to take my time, I punched in Duane's number and set the phone to speaker.

"Hey, sweetheart," his voice always made my inside quiver.

"I'm headed to the high school for a meeting. Can I bring you a coffee?"

"Sure, and one of those apple scones. I'll be in the coach's office for the next half hour before my first class starts."

"See you in fifteen. Love you."

"Ditto."

I hung up, my face hurting from the grin that stretched my cheeks. Since we'd set a wedding date for three months' time, I was almost afraid he might not be as excited to see me all the time. I was wrong. If anything, setting the date made our time together even more precious.

We weren't planning anything elaborate, just a small ceremony by the lake. River Valley had a wonderful clubhouse that overlooked the water so we wouldn't have to worry about the weather. I actually hoped it would snow and was having Mom make me a furred shawl, just in case.

A parking spot in front of the coffee shot beckoned as if it were waiting for me. I pulled in and cut the ignition, my taste buds eager for their first sip of a frozen mocha coffee. Duane preferred his coffee black. Blech. Chocolate made everything better.

I ordered my usual, Duane his preference, and two scones, one apple and one cream cheese. Treats in hand, I returned to my car and drove to the school. Parking was scarce, but I found a vacant visitor spot. Hands full, I entered the front doors and signed in, collecting my volunteer badge. Ugh. I hadn't known they'd take the picture the day I did my fingerprints and I'd had on my trusty overalls and my hair pulled back into a ponytail. Sometimes, I was just too lazy to take the time to gussy up. And, I always ended up regretting those times.

When I reached Duane's office, he rushed forward to keep me from dropping something. "Thanks. This will hit the spot."

"Crazy morning already?" I sat in a plastic chair across from his desk.

He nodded. "School in session only a week and I already have a first string player ineligible to play the first game because of fighting."

"But the first game is weeks away."

"That the best discipline I could think of. After school detention doesn't work for these guys. They sit and text under their desk where the monitor can't see them."

I nodded and sipped my drink, knowing from personal experience how ineffective detention was. Instead of texting, we passed notes. "I'm meeting with Mrs. Grimes about helping with the book fair."

Duane winced. "My condolences. She's worse than ever, but seems to be in a good mood today."

"I hope you're right." I blew him a kiss and left his office. The library was positioned across from the administration office so I retraced my steps.

"Good morning, Mrs. Steele." Principal Dean pushed his glasses up his nose. "Solved any murders lately?" He laughed, the sound more of a guffaw then anything.

"Not today." I'd never liked the man. He should have retired years ago along with the librarian. Wasn't there an age limit to working with kids? What this school needed was an up-to-date principal. Someone who knew the issues today's students faced. Someone other than the Barbie doll of a vice-principal, Sheri Hopkins. I watched as Mr. Dean's gaze followed the VP across campus.

I knew her type. She was more interested in being the kids' friend rather than authority figure. There were bound to be several teenage boys with a crush on her. Who could take her seriously with her mound of blond hair and tight skirts?

I sighed and pushed open the door to the library, immediately taking a deep breath, pulling in the wonderful aroma of books. Large metal crates occupied the far section, book fair stuff most likely. I thought book fairs didn't go past elementary school.

"It's about time you showed up." Mrs. Grimes stepped out of the back room, her arms full of pamphlets. "I need these sorted into class amounts and distributed into teachers' mailboxes.

"Good morning to you, too, Mrs. Grimes. It's been a long time."

She peered over the top of her glasses. "You haven't changed much, and your daughter is a chip off the old block."

"Me or her father's?"

"Both." She thrust the papers into my arms, almost making me drop my drink. That would have been a very bad thing. "You can sit anywhere. Put them in stacks of thirty."

"I thought I was here to help with the book fair."

"Those are for the book fair. Open house is next week, and we need to be prepared. Families will be bringing their younger students, and they will want to buy books." She sat at her desk, hiding behind a stack of books that looked too old to belong to the school library.

I shrugged. I'd heard she collected antique books. Maybe she did some of her collecting while at work. It was none of my business. I grinned. As if that ever stopped me from poking my nose where it didn't belong.

The jingle of keys drew my attention back to Mrs. Grimes. She had a sly smile on her face as she placed a yellowed piece of paper in a drawer and locked it. She turned in a circle, the key in her hand. When she caught me looking, she ducked into the back room.

What was in the drawer? I sipped my coffee, my attention riveted on what could be in her desk. What was so important she felt it necessary to hide the key rather than keep it on the lanyard around her neck?

We pretty much ignored each other for the time it took me to count out the rest of the papers. When I'd finished, I told her I'd be back, and she grunted that she'd heard me. Whatever. I wouldn't let her mood spoil my day. One more hour of volunteer time, and I'd be back at Country Gifts from Heaven. My home away from home.

"Mom?" Lindsey stopped so fast, the boy in back of her almost fell. "What are you doing here?"

"Volunteering in the library, didn't I tell you?"

"You did not. Please pretend we don't know each other." With a scowl, she continued on her way.

I didn't let her attitude bother me. She loved me, and I wasn't about to embarrass her in front of her classmates. I hoped.

Four teachers sat in the teacher's lounge, assorted beverages on the table in front of them. Lynn glanced up. "How's it going?"

"Fine. Why is the high school having a book fair? Haven't these kids outgrown this sort of thing?" I began slipping the assorted piles into cubbies.

"Mrs. Grimes wants to encourage the older students to read more. She said she'll be carrying more age appropriate books and activities." Lynn sipped a diet soda. "As an English teacher, I applaud her efforts."

Another teacher, I believe she taught history, laughed. "That old bat just wants to draw attention to herself. I doubt it'll do any good."

"Marsha, this is Estelle Willis, our resident pessimist and budding author." Lynn tossed her can into a recycling bin.

"You've heard what she'd involved herself in lately, haven't you?" Estelle crossed her arms over her more than ample chest and glanced around the table.

"I haven't heard anything. But then, I'm stuck in the band room most of my days." A male teacher shrugged.

"She's going around informing people that she's uncovered a treasure. At our book club last night, she told us all that she found a map in one of the old books she bought. Seriously? A treasure map?" She stood and speared me with a glance. "Why don't you see if you can get to the bottom of that, Ms. Super Sleuth?" With those words, she lumbered out of the lounge.

"What did I do?" I set the last of the fliers in the boxes. "I'm just minding my own business."

"Don't worry," Lynn said. "Grimes and Estelle have been feuding for years." She winked. "I think it's over Mr. Dean."

"Eeew." My few hours a week at the school promised to either be disgusting or entertaining. I'd reserve judgment for now.

Not in a hurry to return to the library, I headed for the staff restroom. One can only stall for so long between taking care of business, washing hands, and fluffing hair. There was nothing left to do but head back to the library.

"Marsha?" Janet Snyder, PTO president, halted me in the hall. "What can I do to convince you to join the organization?"

"Absolutely nothing." I continued on my way as fast as my legs would carry me.

She scampered after me in ridiculously high heels. "Think of the benefit to the school, to your daughter."

"I'm volunteering time, that's all River Valley High needs from me." I paused with my hand on the door. "Are you seriously here to pester me?"

"Not just you." She shook her head. "But our numbers are shrinking."

I sighed and ducked into the library. Mrs. Grimes wasn't at her desk. Good. I'd have a few minutes of peace before she gave me something else to do.

When thirty minutes passed and there was no sign of her, I decided to check the back room. After all, the woman had to be pushing seventy years of age. Maybe she fell asleep.

Sure enough, she sat at a battered old desk, her face resting on the wood. "Mrs. Grimes?"

Her head lolled to the side. She'd been strangled with her floral scarf.

2

After checking for a pulse and not finding one, I backed out of the room and slammed the door. How did I constantly find myself in these messes? I peeked through the window at the poor woman, and then rushed to the phone on her desk to ring the office manager.

"This is Sarah." Her nasally voice made me cringe. Sarah Boatwright, an attractive woman in her mid-thirties had the voice of a saw.

"This is Marsha Steele. Mrs. Grimes is dead."

"Excuse me?"

"Dead. In her storeroom." My pulse pounded in my head.

"But the bell is about to ring?"

"Seriously?! Are you insane? Call the police." There might be a door separating me from the corpse, but that wasn't nearly enough of a barrier. Not that I expected Mrs. Grimes to turn into a zombie and chase me down the hall, but still.

"No, I mean, the library is about to be flooded with students." Sarah sighed. "You have to block the door. I'm making the call to the police now." She hung up.

I replaced the receiver and spun in a circle. Block the door with what? I wasn't big enough or strong enough to hold out thirty-five teenagers. The book fair crates. I sprinted across the room and pushed. The thing weighed a ton. I put my shoulder into it and pushed with my legs. Inch by excruciating inch, I managed to block one of the double doors. How much time did I have?

I rushed to move the second one, getting it into place as the bell rang. Moments later, someone banged on the door. I leaned against the crate to catch my breath, realizing then that I was now blocked in with a dead body. My legs refused to hold me, and I slid to the floor.

"Mrs. Grimes? Why's the door locked?" A girl's voice drifted through my barricade.

"Something is blocking the door." A boy said. "Me and a couple of the guys can push it open."

"No!" I lunged to my feet. "You can't come in. There's been a, uh, toxic chemical spill. Yeah."

"In the library? Who is this?"

The crates moved. How was it possible that a couple of kids could move what took me a superhuman strength to budge?

"Go get the principal."

"Are you holding Mrs. Grimes hostage?"

"Yeah, that's it." Silly kids.

Soon shouts that Mrs. Grimes was in the hands of a terrorist vibrated down the halls. I shook my head and leaned against the crate. I pulled out my cell phone and pressed in Duane's number. It went to voice mail. Of course he won't answer during class.

"Mrs. Steele?" Principal Dean knocked on the door. "I need you to let me in."

Finally, help had arrived. I shoved against the crate until it moved just enough for him to squeeze through.

"The police are on their way," he said. "I need to unlock the side door so they can get in."

There was a side door? I could have gotten out at any time. No, that would have left the poor librarian alone.

He glanced at the store room door as he made his way to another door behind a bookshelf. Finished, he stood next to me. "She's in there?"

"Yes. Strangled with her scarf."

"Are you sure she's dead?"

"Of course I'm sure. I wouldn't have called the front office if she weren't."

"What about the students?"

"We sent the ones outside the door to the gym." Mr. Dean rubbed his chin. "I'm not sure how to proceed here. We've never had a murder at the school before. Assaults, yes, but no one has ever been killed."

"The police will handle it. I've had experience with these things." Right. I usually ended up in harm's way with someone holding a gun to my head.

"That's right. Our resident mystery solver." Mr. Dean tried to smile, and failed. Instead, the attempt looked more like a grimace.

"I should have known Marsha would be here."

Bruce Bennett, our very own Barney Fife, waltzed into the library with an officer I'd never met. "This is Officer Bradford, the rookie on our force."

I already felt sorry for the guy. No one should have to work that close with Bruce. "Nice to meet you, I think. She's behind that door."

"Mrs. Steele found her," Mr. Dean said.

"Of course she did." Bruce opened the door, and the four of us stared at the body. He exhaled deeply and waved the rookie in first. "Check out the scene. Where is that ambulance?"

Not that she needed one, but I guessed it would be better if she left covered by a sheet rather than the student body getting a glimpse of her face. My hands shook, and I grabbed the teacher rolling chair.

"Don't touch anything." Bruce shook his head.

"I've already touched the door handle, the desk over there and this one, the phone, and those two crates. Oh, yeah, and her neck."

"For crying out loud, Marsha. What are you doing here anyway?"

"Volunteering to help with the book fair." I guess my time would be finished now. No librarian, no book fair. Unless … I glanced at the locked drawer. What if someone killed her for what was in that drawer?

No, Duane would kill me. Still, I couldn't help but wonder 'what if', especially after hearing the conversation in the teacher's lounge. People thought Mrs. Grimes had something of value and experience had taught me that some people thought that a good enough reason to kill.

"Do you feel up to continuing the book fair,

Mrs. Steele?" Mr. Dean leaned against the desk. "Mrs. Grimes felt passionate about it, and the school could use the funds. It could be a tribute to the poor woman. I don't think it will hurt anything if we move the date back two weeks. Have it around Halloween?"

"Oh." Question answered. Duane couldn't be too upset if I snooped around while fulfilling a dying woman's wish, right? "Of course." How difficult could a book fair be?

The ambulance arrived and carted Mrs. Grimes' body away. I sighed and stood, unsure of what to do next. "I suppose there's a lot of work left to do."

"Yes. All the information for the fair is in that box." Mr. Dean pointed.

"Nothing is removed and whatever it is you're talking about will have to wait until we've done our investigation." Bruce shook his head. "Marsha, you've been involved in enough crimes that you should know this."

"But she died in that room, not the main library."

"Doesn't matter. Go home and I'll be along in a while to take your statement."

He'd taken enough statements from me over the last few months to make a book. I grabbed my purse, and the box of fair information, and then stormed out the side door. A group of students, Lindsey included, congregated in the parking lot. Wasn't anyone in class?

"Mom? Were you held hostage by the terrorist, too?" Lindsey rushed forward.

"There was no terrorist. I found Mrs. Grimes

dead."

"Again? What is wrong with you?" She withdrew, shooting daggers from her eyes while in the protection of her friends.

"I have no idea, sweetie. See you at supper." I sashayed past the gawking teens as if I didn't have a care in the world when in all actuality my insides shook like the San Madres fault.

I sat in my car and waited while they wheeled Mrs. Grimes's body out on a gurney. Although she was a mean-spirited old woman most of the time I'd known her, it was sad to think someone had closed the last chapter on her life.

I pulled into the alley behind Country Gifts from Heaven and carried the book fair box into the store with me. Mom waited on a customer, so I stuck the box, and my purse, under the counter before reaching for one of the ruffled aprons Mom insisted we wear. She swore it added character to the store. I thought it made us look ridiculous.

"What's in the box?" she asked once the customer left.

"Stuff for the book fair. I'm in charge of it now."

"Mrs. Grimes doesn't have time?"

"Not really." I leaned against the counter. "Someone killed her this morning while I was in the teacher's lounge. Principal Dean put me in charge of the fair."

"Back up." Mom held up her hand. "Somebody killed the librarian in the library?" She rubbed her nose. "Sounds like the plot of a really bad book."

"Yeah, they choked her with the silk flowered

scarf she wore."

"And now, you can't stay out of things if you wanted to, which I'm sure you won't, because the principal asked you to continue there until...?"

"Halloween."

"Of course." Mom shook her head. "So, how do you propose to pull all this off without getting yourself killed?"

"I'm not sure." I plopped into one of the wooden rocking chairs we had available for purchase. "Right now, I'm going to focus on a Halloween themed book fair and how to sell lots of books for the school. Then, I'm tearing up my volunteer badge."

"Don't be so dramatic." Mom grabbed a rag from the pocket of her apron and started dusting shelves. "You should take a cruise. It was the best thing me and Leroy did."

I had no idea what Duane had planned for a honeymoon. All he would tell me was that he wanted it to be a surprise. Personally, I was hoping for a European tour. But, before I could focus my mind on that pleasant trip, I had to get through the next month.

Maybe Lindsey could help me plan a book fair that high school students would actually enjoy. I grabbed some quilt pieces and thread, ready to finish a lap quilt to sell in the shop. Since Mom's marriage to Leroy a few months ago, she'd turned over most of the running of our business to me. While it also increased my share of the profits, it almost doubled the amount of work I had to do. Now, add in the book fair, and I was swamped.

"Why don't we sell some crafts on consignment?"

Mom stopped dusting. "Not sell our own things?"

"We'd still do that, but it would lessen the burden of having to provide all the stock ourselves. We could be choosey about what we put on consignment, only using things that meet our standards."

"Let me think about it." Mom resumed her work, her brow creased.

She took a lot of pride in selling only what we made, but the chore of keeping the shelves full was almost more than I could handle alone. It had been months since Mom had sewed anything. We already sold yarn and craft books. Having a consignment corner wouldn't be too far of a stretch.

"Okay." Mom gave a definitive nod. "But we have to be very picky about what goes on our shelves. Put that quilt down. I want to get some Halloween type things finished this week."

"Oh, goody." I moved to the storeroom and pulled a foam pumpkin off the shelf. I'd carve something cute, rather than scary, and put them on display in the front window. Folks who wanted to keep their jack-o-lanterns for more than a few days should buy them faster than I could carve.

I caught sight of a felt witch's hat and a time out baby with a chainsaw. I knew exactly what I'd do for the upcoming book fair. A haunted house. Visitors would have to enter the haunted halls in order to reach the books at the end.

It should be fun for everyone. Except me. I hated haunted houses. What if one of the people in costume were really a deranged killer using the haunted house for their own evil purpose?

3

"A haunted house?" Mr. Dean tapped his forefinger on his chin "We try to not highlight any religious holiday, Mrs. Steele."

"Halloween isn't a religious holiday." Seriously? "If we want the students to enter the book fair, we need something to appeal to their age group. They seem to flock to that haunted corn maze every year. This is right up their alley. Student council and the PTO—a"

"PTSO," he said. "The name has been changed to Parent Teacher Student Association. We don't want to leave anyone out."

Of course not. He probably gave all members of the football team a participation trophy, too. "Then I should have more than enough help. We'll need to get started right away."

He nodded. "Let my secretary know and she'll put it in the announcements. When do you want to start?"

"Monday." That gave me the weekend to finalize more of the details.

He rubbed his hands together, a wicked gleam

in his eye that had me sitting straighter in my chair. "I want to participate, too. This should be fun."

I sure hoped so. I stepped out of his office and into the small room next door. Cheryl Wright, a former classmate of mine and the principal's secretary, sat hunched over her keyboard. The sound of clicking keys filled the room. "Good morning, Cheryl."

"Hey, Marsha." She sat back and raised red-rimmed eyes in my direction. "What can I get for you?"

"I guess you've heard I'm in charge of the book fair."

She nodded as tears welled. She reached for a Kleenex. "I don't know how you can do it. Poor Mrs. Grimes. To meet such a fate, why I cry every time I think of it."

To my recollection, Cheryl cried over just about everything. In school, she'd cried at hearing the school's fight song, over every sport loss, and every time someone read a poetry assignment in English class. Not to take anything away from her mourning Mrs. Grimes, but I had a hard time digging up any compassion. "It was a horrible thing."

"And you were the one to find her." She fluttered a hand toward me. "You poor thing."

"Yes, well…Mr. Dean sent me in here to ask you to announce that I am looking for student council members to volunteer for a haunted house I'm putting on to draw attention to the book fair."

"I can do that. What fun." Her withdrawn face said she thought it anything but fun.

"We'll have the book fair the two nights before

Halloween. I'll have some fliers made up and put them on the counter in the front office. Will that be all right?"

"Perfect." She turned back to her computer.

Dismissed, I headed to the front office. Janet Snyder, head of the PTO, no PTSO, stood chatting with the attendance clerk. "Just the person I wanted to see." I grinned. "I'm looking for volunteers." I explained my plan for the book fair.

Her eyes widened. "A haunted house at a school? Mr. Dean approved this?" She shook her head. "I don't celebrate Halloween."

"Maybe not, but the majority of the students do." I still had tons of high school age kids ringing my doorbell every year. "Maybe you could work the book fair aspect and leave the other to the students?"

"I could do that. But all the decorations will give me the heebie jeebies. You should also ask Mrs. Grimes's book club members to help out as a tribute to her. They're older women, but they could do some of the more menial type tasks."

"That's a good idea, thanks. Have the police opened the library yet?"

"It's only been a day. Give them time."

"Then do you know how to get in touch with the book club?" I cocked my head. Who got her panties in a wad?

She scribbled a number on a piece of paper. "Here's the phone number for Norma Rae Jennings. Mrs. Grimes was head of the club, but Norma Rae is the second-in-command."

"Thanks." I shoved the paper into my pocket.

Instead of calling, it might be more beneficial to join the club and get to know the other women before blurting out my request over the phone. As if I had time for one more thing. Maybe I could get Mom to join instead.

My cell phone rang as I crossed the parking lot. I smiled to see Duane's face pop on the screen. "Hey."

"How's your morning? I'm between classes and thought I'd give you a call."

I unlocked the door to my Prius and slid inside. "It's going okay. I'm finalizing some details on the book fair."

"Yeah, I've heard of the haunted house. I'd like to be a part of that."

"Really? That would be awesome! You can be the chainsaw wielding maniac."

"Perfect. See you at dinner. Love you."

We hung up, and I drove back to the shop. Having Duane present would help keep the students' shenanigans at a minimum. None of the boys would want to anger the football coach.

Bruce and the new officer strode across the parking lot and entered the library from the side door. What could they possibly have left to do? I really wanted access to the locked drawer.

I slid from the car, locked it, and ducked inside the library side entrance before anyone could stop me. Bruce and Officer Bradford were in the back room where Mrs. Grimes was killed. I needed to find the key to that drawer, and fast.

The low murmurs of their voices propelled me to search through desk drawers. I was most likely searching for a small gold key, the type used for filing cabinets. What if she'd worn it around her neck? I didn't remember seeing a lanyard. Would the office manager have an extra key?

Wait. She'd had the key in her hand when she'd ducked into the back room. I bit my bottom lip. I couldn't go in there with Bruce.

"What are you doing here? We haven't allowed access to the library yet." Bruce marched toward me.

"The side door was open. I need some things, like—" I searched around for something, anything, and grabbed a notebook off the desk. "Notes."

His lips thinned. "That's my notebook." He held out his hand. "You'll have access to the library again tomorrow."

I handed over the book and tried to peer around him. "What are y'all looking for?"

"That's none of your business."

"But I need something out of there."

"Tomorrow." He pointed at the door.

"Fine." I whirled and headed back to my car. What a waste of time that had been. If Mrs. Grimes had stuck the key in a pocket or her purse, I'd never get my hands on it. All that would be handed off to the next of kin. Who was her next of kin? I drummed my fingers on the steering wheel. Her personal effects had to go somewhere.

I didn't know why, exactly, but I knew whatever was locked in that drawer had a bearing on her death. Call it a snoopy woman's intuition. I started the car and drove to the shop. I had giant spiders to make. I'd decided I really didn't like Halloween.

Who came up with the stupid so-called holiday anyway? Within a couple of days' time, I found myself neck deep in darkness.

I should have chosen a harvest theme for the book fair, but that wouldn't attract the traffic we needed. I owed it to Mrs. Grimes to put on the best book fair the school had ever had.

I entered the shop to the sight of customers standing four deep at the counter. Not one of them had anything in their hands to purchase. At the jingle of the door, they all turned.

"There she is!" They rushed me.

I stumbled backward onto the sidewalk. My feet slid out from under me. I landed in an unbecoming heap on my backside.

"You found Mrs. Grimes?" An elderly woman held out her hand. The strength in her arms as she helped me to my feet belied her frail appearance. "I'm Ingrid Jennings. This is my daughter, Norma Rae. Harriet was the president of our book club."

Harriet? How did I not know Mrs. Grimes's first name after all these years?

"We heard you were with her in her final moments."

"I was." I dusted off the back of my denim jeans, hoping I hadn't knocked one of the sparkly sequins off. Some days seemed to scream for the overalls I used to wear.

"How was she? Did she say anything about her dear friends?" Ingrid cocked her head, much like a bird.

"No, she put me to work." I pushed past them and took sanctuary behind the counter. "What do they want?" I hissed at Mom.

She shrugged. "You. They're all nothing but Nosey Nellies."

The crowd followed me back inside. "Oh, no." Through the window, I spotted my nemesis, Stacy Tate, resident reporter of River Valley.

She elbowed her way through the women. "Well, well. It looks like Marsha is knee deep in trouble again."

"I thought you left town after the last fiasco." The woman had almost been killed by the deranged ex-wife of a man she'd cheated with.

"I only took a leave of absence." Stacy pulled a notebook from the oversized red leather bag she carried. "May I interview you? Thanks. Tell us what you found in the high school library."

"Lots of books." I would not make this easy for her.

"Marsha." She narrowed her eyes. "Wouldn't you rather have a friend interview you? We miss you at the paper. Your gossip column was the hit of the town."

What a liar. Since the moment I spilled the beans about her breast enhancement surgery, Stacy had been out to get me. "I wasn't in the library when Mrs. Grimes was killed. I found her after returning from the teacher's lounge." I shuddered.

Stacy's pen flashed silver as it scratched across the pad. "Were you frightened? What did the victim look like? Can you tell us how she was killed?"

Even I knew not to give out too much information. If I said something, even inadvertently about the murder, Bruce would slap handcuffs on me faster than a hummingbird's wings fluttered. The man was only waiting for his chance.

"She looked dead." I crossed my arms. "You know I can't divulge any facts."

At the word dead, the onlookers gasped. What? They thought she'd look like Sleeping Beauty? "Ladies, we have work to do. If you aren't going to make a purchase, we need to ask you to leave. You're keeping paying customers from entering the store."

No one waited outside, but I didn't need an audience when dealing with Stacy. She usually left me feeling, and looking, like a fool. Lord, give me patience.

Ingrid rushed forward and slipped a pink sheet of paper in my hand. "We have a club meeting tonight. We hope you can join us. You, too, Gertie." She led the group from the store.

"Are you going to solve this mystery like you did the other two?" Stacy's eyes gleamed.

4

"Supper was delicious, as always." I carried mine and Duane's plates to the kitchen sink, Mom's lasagna resting in my stomach. Mom and Leroy may have moved to the guesthouse, letting Lindsey and I live in the main house, but she still did most of the cooking. Of which I was grateful. My tendencies to—experiment—in the kitchen, often led to a disastrous meal.

"What are you two up to tonight?" Duane came up behind me and nuzzled my neck. "Usually you're in your slippers by now."

"Mom and I are trying out a book club." I closed my eyes and leaned into him.

He stiffened. "The one Mrs. Grimes ran?" At my nod, he sighed. "You're getting involved."

I turned in his embrace and stared up into his dark blue eyes. "I didn't ask to be. Mr. Dean asked me to continue the book fair and Ingrid Jennings invited Mom and I to come tonight. What could it hurt? It's a bunch of old ladies."

"Have you forgotten you were almost killed by an old lady a few months ago?"

He was talking about the last murder I'd dabbled in. "She had help from her son."

He cupped my face. "Don't get yourself killed before our wedding."

"I won't." I stood on tip-toe to kiss him.

"Let's go. We don't want to be late." Mom bustled into the kitchen. "Y'all can smooch later. Duane, are you staying to keep Leroy company? I think there's a game on TV."

"Sure. I never turn down the opportunity to watch football on a big screen." He hugged me. "Be careful."

"Seriously, it's just a book club meeting."

He didn't look convinced, but left me and Mom to our devices. "I'll drive." Mom drove her big Cadillac like a torpedo. If Duane needed to worry about anything, it was me getting into Mom's car.

Five minutes later we were headed to church where the meeting was held. Most people seemed to book the fellowship hall for one event or another. I'd always thought book clubs were held in people's homes. How many members were there to warrant the big hall?

I pulled into the parking lot between the only two cars there. I glanced at Mom. "Big crowd."

She shrugged and opened her door. "Let's get this over with. What book are they discussing?"

I had no idea. Ingrid hadn't said in her note. "I'm sure this is for us to get acquainted with the other members."

"Or to grill you for information about Harriet."

Mom was probably right. When there was a new mystery in town, I suddenly became very popular.

We exited the Prius and headed up the walk.

Flowers lined the cement path. Our shoes beat out a muffled rhythm. A mockingbird serenaded from a nearby oak tree. A beautiful autumn night, and I was willingly going into a lair of nosey women to spoil the evening. What I'd rather be doing was snuggling with Duane on the couch.

"She's here!" A shrill voice called from the fellowship hall.

Mom and I stepped into the brightly lit room. Ingrid and Norma Rae Jennings and Cheryl Wright, Mr. Dean's secretary, grinned at us. They sat around a round table, books in front of them. What a crowd.

Ingrid stood and rushed our way. "Have a seat, ladies. We're discussing which book we'd like to read next. October is horror month. We're thinking about reading something that has to do with zombies."

My steps faltered. Who were these women? I glanced at Mom. She cast me a wide-eyed glance.

"Zombies?" She mouthed.

I shook my head and sat in one of the empty chairs. Lindsey had just read a story she raved about. A zombie novella by a Spanish author. At least I knew of one title to recommend. Not that I'd read it of course. I preferred romantic suspense.

"Cheryl, would you call roll, please?" Ingrid took her seat.

Three present members and they did a roll call? When Cheryl called Harriet's name, they all bowed their heads.

"Harriet was really looking forward to horror

month," Norma Rae said. "It was her favorite genre. That and mystery."

I kept my mouth shut, biting my tongue to keep from saying how she'd fallen into her own horror plot. What was wrong with me? I tended to giggle or blurt out nonsense when I was nervous. It was safer not to say anything.

"Next on our agenda…we'd like to welcome our guests." Ingrid clapped. "We're always looking for new blood." She laughed. "We like to inject the spirit of whatever genre we're reading into our meetings."

I glanced at my watch. The meetings took two hours? We'd been there less than fifteen minutes.

"Now," Ingrid leaned her elbows on the table. "Before we get started…Marsha, tell us about Harriet's last moments. What did she say? What did she do?"

"I, uh, hmm." I fiddled with the silver studs on my purse. "She handed me a pile of book fair fliers and asked me to put them in teacher's boxes."

"True," Cheryl said. "I witnessed her doing just that, along with a couple of the teachers. Go on."

"She was…gone when I got back."

"Gone? Where?" Ingrid's brows rose. Her forehead wrinkled. "Oh!" She frowned. "Where were her belongings? We know she was cataloguing a new shipment of antique books. She told us."

"I think those are still in the library. Officer Barnett said I could return tomorrow. Was there something in particular you were looking for?" Like a yellowed piece of paper, maybe?

"We were going to discuss reading Bram

Stoker's Frankenstein this month. Harriet said that book was in the shipment." She sighed. "I guess that's out of the question now."

"I think you mean Dracula," Mom stated.

"Oh, yes." Ingrid's lips thinned. "How silly of me. I'm so distraught over this whole thing."

"Did Mrs. Grimes have any next of kin?" I sat my purse, now minus a stud from my picking at it, on the floor. "I'm sure the books should go to them."

Norma Rae shook her head. "Not that she spoke of. At our last meeting, she spoke of a treasure. We assumed she meant the books. I think the books should go to the members of this club. After all, we were her dearest friends."

"We're getting off track," Cheryl said. She tapped a pencil on the papers in front of her. "We're supposed to be discussing our next read."

I gave them the name of the book Lindsey read. They agreed it would be perfect. Mom said they should go ahead with Dracula, but the idea was shot down. Cheryl said it would be too painful to read page-after-page of a book that would only remind her of Harriet.

Thoroughly confused, I chewed the inside of my lip, wishing for my M&Ms. The club members spoke of mourning Harriet, but their actions showed anything but. The Jennings ladies were more interested in Harriet's antique books. Cheryl was absorbed by the choosing of their next read. The fact that Harriet had supposedly mentioned a treasure hadn't escaped me, either. Money was always a big factor in murder. In fact, it had been the motive for the first mystery I'd found myself immersed in.

Did any of these three women have need for a large sum of money? Of course, the treasure could actually be one of the old books. Antiques were worth quite a lot in some circles. Besides searching for a key, I'd be online tomorrow looking up the worth of Harriet's latest shipment. If I could find a motive for her murder, I might be able to find the culprit, without putting myself in harm's way.

After snacks of too tart lemonade and stale cookies, Mom and I said our goodbyes and headed for the car. Behind the wheel, I stared at the open door of the fellowship room. "That was the strangest meeting."

"What did you expect?" Mom hooked her seatbelt. "They're all a bunch of kooks more interested in books than the fact one of their friends was murdered."

"So you picked up on that, too."

"Of course. I'm not blind."

"What do the Jennings women do?"

"They own a tea room on Main Street." Mom glanced at me. "Why?"

"I'm not sure. Something about the books doesn't ring true." I turned on the ignition and backed from the parking spot. "I'm probably paranoid, but any time the subject of money comes up after someone died, I get suspicious."

"Don't be silly. It's a book club. Of course they're interested in old books."

"The first morning I volunteered, I caught Mrs. Grimes locking up what appeared to be an old sheet of paper. What if the treasure she found is exactly that? A treasure map."

"They don't exist."

"Says who?" I pulled onto the highway and headed toward home.

"Says anybody who's ever gone looking for one. I know you want to solve Harriet's death, but no one at that meeting seemed to have a motive. I'd look at the people who worked with her."

"The teachers?"

Mom nodded. "She had a tendency to make people mad."

True. I remembered when I'd gotten in trouble for losing a library book my senior year, and Mrs. Grimes threatened to keep me from walking at graduation until the book was found or replaced. Mom had been livid.

Headlights appeared in my rearview mirror. I tilted the mirror to get the glare out of my eyes. Why did people insist on keeping their brights on when other cars were around.

Who would want to kill a librarian on the verge of retirement? My suspect list was endless if I included the teachers. I supposed I'd have to include at least half of the student body. It wasn't just parents she irritated.

A ram on the Prius' bumper sent the car skidding. "What the heck?" I pressed the gas and glared at the car behind us.

Mom turned to glance over her shoulder. "They're tailgating a little too close."

"You think? They just rear-ended us." I readjusted my mirror and continued to increase our speed. The car kept pace. "Can you make out who is behind the wheel?"

"I can't even tell what color the car is." Mom tightened her seatbelt. "You've done it again, Marsha. Gotten us into a fix."

"I haven't even started investigating yet."

"No, but folks around here know you will. It's only a matter of time." She screamed as the next jolt threw her forward.

The screech of metal on metal set my teeth on edge. I gripped the wheel and did my best to keep us on the road. "Now would be a good time to start praying."

"I already have." She fumbled in her purse. "I'm calling Leroy."

"You should probably call the police."

"I want to talk to my husband before I die."

I rolled my eyes. "We aren't going to die." I bit my lip at the next jarring jolt and skid onto the road's shoulder. I wanted to talk to Duane. Feel his lips on mine, his arms around me.

The next ram sent us farther off the road. Mom yelped and dropped her phone. She fumbled with her seatbelt.

"Do not take off your seat belt." I yanked the steering wheel in an attempt to keep us from sliding into the ditch. If we stopped, we were at the mercy of the person behind us.

"I can't reach it." She stretched for the phone.

"Hello? Gertie?" Leroy's voice came from the phone on the floor.

"Call the police!" Mom bent to put her mouth as close to the phone as possible. "Someone is trying to kill us."

"Where are you?"

"The road from church. Tell Duane that Marsha loves him."

Oh, good grief. Another yank of the wheel and we spewed gravel. The tires spun, finally gaining traction and propelling us back onto the highway. I wanted to fist bump to our success.

The car behind us slowed, then shot forward. My head snapped back from the impact. My hands released their hold on the wheel. We spun. The massive trunk of an oak tree loomed in front of us.

"Tree!" Mom covered her eyes.

I closed my eyes and crossed my arms in front of my face.

5

I opened my eyes to the sound of sirens. "Mom?"

"I'm still here." She tugged at her seatbelt. "Barely. The belt cut off my breathing for a second. Are you all right?"

"I think so." All my joints worked at least. A pain shot through my chest. We'd both sport bruises by morning.

The front of my car sat against my knees. The steering wheel twisted upward. I guessed it could've been worse, but I loved this car. The insurance company would total it for sure. I blinked back tears, thankful to be alive, and unhooked my seatbelt. I shoved against the door. Stuck tight.

"Stay still, ma'am." A paramedic who didn't look older than my daughter stuck his arm through the now non-existent window and patted my shoulder. "We'll have you out in a jiffy."

"Free my mother first."

"Oh, no, dear. You first. I'm fine. I think I'll take a nap while we wait." Blood dripped from a cut on her forehead.

"Don't fall asleep, ma'am," handsome

paramedic said. "You might have a concussion."

"I did hit my head on this window." Her side window sported a round concave in the glass. A spider web of cracks radiated from the center.

While the paramedics cut us out of the car, I leaned back against the headrest. Where was the car that ran us off the road? They could have killed us while we were unconscious. My blood ran cold. I no longer wanted to know Mrs. Grimes's secret. Mom and I could have been killed.

"Gertie!"

"Marsha!"

I turned my head. Duane and Leroy raced down the embankment. Now that my hero had arrived, I let the tears flow. I didn't have to be strong. Duane's shoulders were big enough for both of us.

He reached in the window and cupped my face. "Are you all right?"

"I think so. My knees are jammed against the front of the car, and the seat belt cut into me, but other than that, I'll live."

"Thank, God." He leaned in and kissed me before the paramedics shoved him aside.

Mom was out and folded in Leroy's arms. He escorted her to a waiting ambulance. They'd most likely make us stay overnight for observation. I sighed. I'd seen the inside of a hospital too much over the last year. I really need to rethink this mystery solving hobby of mine.

The emergency personnel pulled me from the car and handed me over to Duane. My legs collapsed, and he scooped me into his arms. "You should be a gurney," he said.

"This is so much nicer." I cradled my head in the curve of his shoulder.

The news van pulled up and I hid my face from Stacy and her stupid camera. She teetered after us on yellow stilettos. "What happened? Can you give us a comment?"

Duane shouldered past her. "Leave us alone, Stacy. Now is not the time."

"But this is news." She jogged alongside us.

"Not today." He carried me to the waiting ambulance, and set me on a gurney next to the one Mom was on. After one more kiss, he stepped back. "We'll meet you at the hospital."

I nodded and kept my gaze on his until the doors closed.

*

Mom and I were assigned to a joint room. Once the doctor's checked us over, Mom with a concussion and me with swollen knees, they allowed Duane and Leroy to join us. Both men stood at the foot of our beds, crossed their arms, and glared.

"What have you two gotten mixed up in now?" Leroy glanced from Mom to me. "I thought you went to a book club meeting at the church."

"We did," I said. "The car that ran us off the road appeared halfway home. We didn't do anything to warrant the attack."

"Where have you been nosing around?" Duane pulled up a mint green vinyl chair.

"Nowhere. Really." I raised the bed to a sitting position. "The ladies at the club asked about the antique books that Mrs. Grimes just got in, but that's all. I haven't spoken to people at the school about anything other than the book fair." Yet. "Obviously, someone knows something I don't, but they think I know."

He shook his head. "That doesn't make sense."

"Neither does someone running us off the road." Usually this type of danger came when I'd dug more into the mystery. Had I inadvertently said something I shouldn't? Stumbled across a clue I couldn't identify?

"Visiting hours are over." A nurse in scrubs that matched the furniture in the room bustled in. "You may return tomorrow at eight."

Duane frowned before leaning over to plant a kiss on my lips. "Get some rest. We'll be here to pick y'all up in the morning. Love you."

"I love you, too." Tears welled. My entire body ached. I didn't want him to go. Stupid hospital rules.

Once the men left, Mom turned on the television. "Might as well watch the news. See if they captured one of our most embarrassing moments."

"Excuse me?" I turned my head to glare. "I did my best to keep us on the road. I'm the one without a car now."

She grinned, the white bandage on her head a striking contrast to her auburn hair. "I know, sweetie. Just making sure you still have some fire left in you. So, what are we going to do now? I know there's a plan whirling in that brain of yours."

"I'm going to find out who did this. It's got to be the same person that killed Mrs. Grimes." I switched to lying on my side so I could see her better. "Do you think my reputation has preceded me?" After all, I'd barely scratched the surface of the murder. Someone was running scared very early in the game.

"I've no doubt." Mom tapped her fingers on the bed rail. "Suspects number in the hundreds, you know. The book club," she counted off on her free hand. "The bunch of looky Lou's in the store, the high school staff…the students."

"I think we can scratch off the elderly ladies, don't you? It would take some strength to choke someone."

Mom looked insulted. "I could choke someone if I wanted to. All you do is tighten the scarf, then tighten some more, then—"

"I get it." The thought of my mother killing someone disturbed me. I supposed anyone from the age of fifty to seventy still had enough power to dig in their heels and hold on to a silk scarf. Still, it was hard to digest. Maybe the pounding in my head kept me from thinking clearly.

"We need to find out who Harriet's enemies are, and I don't mean people who just dislike her. Someone hated her enough to kill."

"Or wanted something she had." My mind clung to the fact there was a clue in the locked drawer that would answer some questions. I had to find that key or a way to jimmy the drawer open. Tomorrow was Friday. I'd head to the school as soon as Duane picked me up. "How much are antique books worth?"

"Some are worth hundreds of dollars, why?"

"That's the only thing of value I know Mrs. Grimes had. You don't think she has a fortune stashed somewhere, do you? Maybe she let it slip to someone?"

"Maybe." Mom shrugged. "We need to narrow our suspect list down to a manageable few."

"I have a PTO meeting tomorrow night. I'll ask around."

"And put another target on your back."

"How else are we supposed to find out anything? You can't ask the group that rents the back room for their crafts. They've never mentioned knowing Mrs. Grimes, and you know they gossip about just about anyone." A few months ago, Leroy had built on a back room for us which we rented to crafty women. That little good deed almost got me killed.

"True, but a couple of them consider themselves sleuths. It doesn't hurt to have other folks poking their noses around."

"No, but if someone else is already nervous, it puts other people besides ourselves in danger." I couldn't do that to the women. Most of them were old enough they lived in the retirement homes.

I settled back on my bed and stared at the ceiling while Mom immersed herself in channel surfing. Soon, my eyelids grew heavy.

*

"No, I'm not taking you to the library today." Duane walked beside the intern pushing me in a wheelchair out of the hospital.

"But, I've got work to do." I gave him my most pleading look.

"You are going to rest until Monday if I have to tie you to a chair." The thunderous look on his face gave me little room for argument.

"Can I at least go to the PTO meeting tonight?" I couldn't get used to the new acronym. "I need to get things moving on the book fair. I promise I'll be sitting very nicely in a chair."

"You'll be putting out feelers."

He knew me so well. "You could always go with me."

"No thanks." He shuddered. "Besides, I have to be at the football game."

Who was the wise guy that scheduled a meeting on a Varsity game night? I always went to the home games to cheer on my favorite coach. I'd bring that up first thing. "Can I go?"

"Like I could really stop you." He tossed me a smile. "Just be careful, okay?"

"I will. I need a car."

He sighed. "We'll stop at the rental place on the way home. I'm sure your insurance company will reimburse you until you can purchase a new one."

The thought of my pretty powder blue Prius being totaled still stabbed at my heart. Before that, I drove a Sonata. I'd loved that car, too. My solving mysteries sure kept the local car dealership in business. "I want something sexy. Like a red Mustang convertible."

"Great. The killer can spot you easier."

The silent intern handed me into Duane's care. With his hand on my elbow, Duane helped me into his truck. I felt fine except for the bruises across my chest and my swollen knees. I waved at Mom and

Leroy and almost fell backward when my knees refused to bend the way they were meant to. My fiancé placed his hands on my ample rear and hoisted me onto the seat. "Thanks. The knees weren't working very well."

"Yet, you want a car to go gallivanting around town." He loped to the driver's side and slid behind the wheel. He drove us across town to the only car rental place in town.

They didn't have any convertibles. Oh, well. The temperature was too chilly for driving with the top down anyway. They gave me the keys to a Ford Fusion. Cute car. If I liked it, maybe that would be the next car someone wrecked for me.

Duane followed as I drove my new ride home. The exertion from driving, coupled with waiting on a very slow service rep to get me the keys, left me trembling from exhaustion. I was more than ready to camp out on the sofa for the rest of the day.

My sweetie fetched me a tall glass of ice, a diet soda, and the remote to the television. "I've got to get to work now. Will you be all right?"

I nodded. "Leroy is bringing Mom here. We'll recuperate together." In fact, they should have beaten us there. "I need my purse."

He handed it to me, kissed me goodbye, and rushed out the door. I punched in Mom's number. "Where are you?"

"In the guest house." She sounded breathless. "I'll be there in a few." She giggled. "Leroy is making me feel better."

Eew! I punched the off button. I'd rather focus on the sight of Mrs. Grimes's bloated face then picture what my stepfather was doing to make my mother feel better.

6

Opting out of taking prescription pain medication, I downed three Ibuprofen with the last of my diet soda and staggered to the bedroom to get ready for the PTSO meeting. No amount of makeup would cover the bruises from last night's accident, so I settled for pulling my hair into a ponytail and donning my most fashionable skinny jeans and a colorful blouse.

If my attacker was in attendance at the meeting, I wanted them to see how battered I could get without quitting. I slapped on some lipstick that matched the rose in my blouse. As I carefully navigated the stairs on swollen knees, Mom entered through the front door. So much for keeping me company all day. She and Leroy still acted like newlyweds, often leaving me in the lurch.

"Are you hungry?" She held up a casserole dish. "Tuna. Is Lindsey home?"

My stomach rumbled. "No, she texted me to say she was eating at a friend's house. She'll be home around seven. Will you stay and wait for her?"

"You don't want me to go to the meeting with

you? I'm a part of this mystery, you know." Mom marched to the kitchen.

I followed. "I didn't know you wanted to go."

She dished out two servings of tuna casserole with crunched potato chips on top. "Of course I do. We're partners. Like Cagney and Lacey or that other show, Rizzo and someone." She waved the spoon as if the names didn't matter. "Or Sherlock and Watson. You're Sherlock, because he's a smart aleck."

"Gee, thanks." I sat at the table while Mom placed my plate in front of me. "We'll have to eat fast. I don't want to be late."

"We have thirty minutes. It's only a ten minute drive. Eat." She sat across from me, her hair poofed over the top of the bandage on her forehead. I tore my gaze away from the way she'd teased her bangs to try and hide the white gauze. Vanity at its finest.

We finished our late dinner and left the house at ten minutes before seven p.m. If we were lucky, we'd walk in right as the meeting started. All eyes would be on us. Because of my sore knees, I relented and let Mom drive. I hated her white beast of a car. People could see us coming a mile away.

Mom squeezed the beast between two compact cars. "I don't know why they don't make bigger parking spots," she said, squeezing her way out the small space available.

"They're trying to encourage people to buy cars that have better gas mileage." Getting out was tricky with my achy body, but eventually we entered the side door of the library.

Ten people turned to stare, among them, Cheryl

Wright, Estelle Willis, the freshman English teacher, Janet Snyder, head of the PTSO, and her husband Brad, who was the band leader. Behind us, Sarah Boatwright, squeezed her way in. That made thirteen members. Not as much as I would have thought considering how many students were in ninth through twelfth grade. Obviously, most parents were like me and too busy to add one more thing to their schedule.

Janet glanced at her watch. "If everyone will be seated, we can get started."

Averting my eyes from the stock room where Mrs. Grimes met her demise, I sat at the oblong table. I glanced around the room. Everything looked much the same as I'd left it. The antique books still sat in a stack on the desk. I should have counted them. Now, there was no way of knowing whether one was missing. The book fair crates were still in front of the main doors, although someone had moved them back a bit to allow entrance.

I zoned out as the minutes from the last meeting were read, only snapping to attention when Janet called my name. "Yes?"

"You had something to discuss with the group?"

"Oh, yes. I'd like to ask for help with this year's book fair. Principal Dean asked me to continue for the sake of Mrs. Grimes and I thought a Haunted House, or tunnel, would be a good way of attracting the attention of high school students."

"While I don't approve of celebrating Halloween," Janet stated. "I do see how this would draw in the students. Today's youth love this type of evil entertainment. What will the PTSO get out of helping?"

I wasn't aware they would want part of the funds. "What do you usually get?"

"We'll want twenty percent. I refuse to dress in costume but will be more than happy to run the cash register." Janet motioned for Cheryl to write her name beside cashier. "The rest of you can help in whatever manner you see fit."

My family didn't celebrate Halloween either, but now that Lindsey was sixteen, she often joined in with her friends in harmless pranks. The Haunted House might be another way of keeping the students from wandering the streets.

"What about flowers for Harriet's funeral?" Cheryl blinked, her eyes glistening. "I motion that we send an arrangement."

Janet glanced around the group. "Is there going to be a service? I wasn't aware she had any family."

Estelle nodded. "A small memorial is being set up by members of the school. I think flowers are a great idea."

"What kind?" Janet shrugged. "We knew very little about her."

I spotted silk daisies in a pot on her desk. "Daisies."

"Very well. Cheryl, write that down." Janet reached for a bottle of water. Her hand shook, spilling some on the table in front of her.

"Are you all right?" I asked.

"This talk of death upsets me."

She didn't seem upset. Instead, she seemed very focused on the topic at hand. I needed to find a way to get all my suspects in one room together. "If it bothers you to hold the meetings here, why not move them? Norma Rae Jennings owns the tea room on Main Street. Maybe she would be glad for the extra business."

Janet's eyes widened. "Hold the PTSO meetings off campus? Is that done?"

"I wouldn't mind," Cheryl said. "This place gives me the creeps now."

Brad glanced up from where he played online gambling on his phone. "Fine with me. I'm only here because Janet drags me. She can force me to attend there as well as here." He bowed his head back over his phone.

"This is my last year anyway," Estelle said. "I've almost got enough money to retire. Once that happens, I'm out of here."

"The loyalty in this room just warms my heart." Janet slapped the phone out of her husband's hands.

Mom and I glanced at each other, both clamping our lips together in an effort not to laugh. River Valley had more than its share of quirky residents.

"I have a question." Mom raised her hand.

"You aren't in a classroom, Gertie." Estelle shook her head.

"I'm just wondering why no one in this room has commented on the way Marsha and I look. Granted, you probably all know that we were run off the road last night." She speared each member with a look as if by doing so, they might confess. "Maybe one of you are responsible."

"Good grief." Sarah banged her palm on the table. "Are you accusing one of us of reckless driving? We are responsible members of society."

"No." Mom stood. "I'm accusing someone of trying to kill me and my daughter." She grabbed her purse. "See y'all at the next meeting." She stormed out the door.

I muttered my apologies and followed as fast as my bruised body would allow. "What this about?"

"Just trying to flush out a bird."

I made note of the models and colors of the cars in the parking lot. If one of them tried to run us off the road, I wanted to know without a doubt who to blame. "Don't you think that made the target on our backs bigger?"

"Yes, so don't tell Leroy." She slid behind the wheel of the Caddy. "He'll make me stop helping you."

Whether or not she was actually helping was debatable. I stared at my reflection in the window on the way home. I did find it curious that no one mentioned the accident. Maybe they thought it would embarrass us? "I think we need to make attending the memorial service a priority."

"I agree. We need to be everywhere at all times until the killer is flushed out of hiding." Mom pulled into the driveway. "You still have your Taser, right?"

"Never leave home without it."

"I bought one myself when Leroy and I were traveling the country." She patted her purse. "I think I need a gun. If we're both armed, no one will mess with us. We'll find some innocent way of letting folks know we have weapons."

Who was this woman? I rarely carried my gun, although I was tickled to death when I found a pink

9-millimeter. I kept it locked and safe on the top shelf of my closet. "Bruce is going to have a heart attack if he finds out you have a gun." I shoved my door open.

"What he doesn't know won't hurt him."

"What are you going to tell Leroy?"

"That I want to start target shooting. He doesn't need to know that the target is someone trying to kill my girl." She grinned at me.

My mama, the she-bear. I understand how she felt, being a mother myself. If someone tried to hurt Lindsey, I wouldn't hesitate to put them in the crosshairs.

We entered the kitchen to the sight of our men and Lindsey playing Chinese checkers. I never could get her to play games with me.

Duane smiled. "How did the meeting go?"

"Good. What are you doing here?" I bent to give him a kiss.

"The other team forfeited. Not enough eligible players."

"Ouch. I should have plenty of help for the book fair."

"You look exhausted." He pulled me into his lap.

"Gross." Lindsey stood. "If you're going to start that, I'm going to my room." She flounced away, sending the four adults into laughter.

"She'll change her mind about that someday," Mom said.

"Not too soon, I hope." Although Lindsey had a boyfriend a few months ago, she still seemed to prefer spending most of her times with her girlfriends. I wasn't naïve enough to believe it wouldn't all change soon.

Duane wanted a child of his own someday. With me pushing thirty-six years old, I guessed we'd have to start right away after getting married. Me, a mother of a new-born with a daughter almost out of high school, starting all over with diapers, potty-training, and hormonal mood swings.

I slid from his lap and headed for the refrigerator. "Anyone thirsty? We have tea."

"No, thanks." Duane stood. "I only stopped by to make sure you made it home safe. Walk me out?"

I followed him to his truck and stepped into his arms. After several minutes of kisses that left me weak, I stepped back. His face was in shadow, yet I knew every angle. "I love you."

"Ditto, beautiful."

"Even with the colorful bruises?"

"Even then. I can't wait until I don't have to leave."

"Darn morality." I grinned.

"Yep." He kissed me again, then got into his truck. "I'll see you in the morning. Maybe we can head to the lake and do some fishing."

I hated fishing, but if it meant spending time with him, I'd go. I stood and watched him back out of the drive. As I turned to head back to the house, car headlights flicked on.

Why was a car sitting on the street with its lights off?

7

Purse over my shoulder, and the swelling in my knees down, I rushed into the front office of the high school, ready to tackle the locked drawer. I signed the volunteer book and grabbed my volunteer badge. With a grin and a wave to Cheryl, I headed down the hall.

"Wait." Cheryl rushed toward me. "Mr. Dean wants a detailed report of what the haunted house will entail."

"He wants it now?"

She nodded. "I'm sorry. I know you have tons of work to do."

Not to mention a drawer to break into. "I don't have all the details, but I'll come up with something."

"Then, once he approves it, he wants a copy in each of the teacher's boxes." She gave an apologetic smile. "He wants me to help you. Do you mind coming to the teacher's lounge?"

I groaned and followed her. It didn't do a lot of good for me to plan anything. Something always got in the way. The last person I wanted to plan something scary with was Cheryl. She'd shiver and get pale at every chainsaw maniac I mentioned. Not that I particularly enjoyed haunted things, but after what I'd gone through the last few months, people in costume weren't frightening. I didn't intend to go through the tunnel of doom anyway. "We'll call it the Tunnel of Doom. Write that down."

She rolled her eyes and sat at a round table in the lounge. "At least let me sit down."

Thankfully, the lounge was empty. We wouldn't have others injecting their ideas.

"Okay, I've written down the name. When we've finished planning, I'll type it up and take it to Mr. Dean for his signature. I'm sure he will also want to participate." She poised her pencil over her pad. "What else?"

"We'll need a lot of black … something. Garbage bags or plastic. Something to make the hall with. I'll have little rooms where something macabre is being acted out. There will also be horrifying monsters lurking around corners and following the attendees." I rubbed my hands together. Kids loved this kind of stuff. "We'll have a tape of scary music playing in the background. There will also be covered boxes that people can stick their hands in to feel something gross."

Cheryl paled with each thing she wrote down. "Are you sure Harriet would have liked this sort of thing?"

"The book club members are the ones who said she loved Dracula." Goodness. We could do something warm and fuzzy but not one high school student would bother to attend. "Isn't the whole point of this to involve the students and make money?"

"Couldn't we do a carnival or something?"

"We could." I'd actually prefer something along that nature. "But how would we get the people with the money to actually make their way to the book fair with dollars still in their pockets?"

"That's the clincher." Cheryl tapped the eraser end of her pencil on the table. "As much as I hate Halloween, it is a good idea. Maybe we could have a happy scarecrow at the end of the tunnel making balloon animals?"

Was she serious? "Uh, if you feel that strongly about it. I actually think you might be on to something." The book fair might be for the high school, but most of the students had younger siblings. "We could do the Tunnel of Doom on a smaller scale and have games put on by the PTSO and student council, a pumpkin patch, bean bag toss, three-legged race, all the old-fashioned fun that kids of today are missing. We'll have a clown making balloon animals right inside the side door to lure in the families with younger kids."

"Now you're talking." Cheryl's pencil raced across the paper. "It's a lot of work to do in a little over three weeks, but if we recruit help now, we can do it. The book club can focus on the inside of the library while everyone else does the tunnel and games."

Excitement over the event finally welled in me. "Since you're at the school every day, why don't you set up a committee and I'll get my stepfather busy on building?"

"Wonderful. I'll type this up right away." She leaped from her chair and dashed out of the lounge, leaving me feeling overwhelmed and relieved at the same time.

I no longer felt as if I were taking on the task alone.

"What are you doing here?" Lynn entered the lounge and stuck two quarters in the vending machine. A diet soda rattled out.

"Planning the book fair with Cheryl. We've come up with something to appeal to all ages." I stood and grabbed my purse. "With the book club, PTSO, and student council, I should have plenty of help."

"If you do too good of a job, they may ask you to take over again in the spring." Lynn laughed and popped the soda top.

I shuddered. "Absolutely not. I have way too much on my plate as it is. Not only do I own a business, but I have a wedding to plan. Not sure how I'm supposed to get all that done with this fair."

"All you need is your dress." Lynn narrowed her eyes. "Right?"

"Yes, I've booked the hall by the lake. Mom is taking care of the food." Thank goodness I wanted a small intimate ceremony with only Lindsey and Lynn standing up for me. Leroy would give me away. "Let's go look for dresses on Saturday, okay?"

"It's a date." She toasted me with her can and left.

Finally, I could head to the library. I glanced at

my watch. Mom was expecting me back at the shop in thirty minutes. I'd have to work fast.

I stepped out of the lounge as the bell rang. Immediately the hall clogged with hundreds of students who didn't care that an adult in a hurry needed to get by. I sighed and waited for the stampede to end. Lindsey strolled by with her arm through the arm of a boy. Interesting. "Hey, Lindsey."

"Mom?" Her cheeks turned pink. "Can't talk now. Got to get to class." She slipped her arm free and fled.

I grinned. Oh, I had a million questions. Relieved she was interested in someone other than the Bobby she had dated last year, I navigated my way to the library and entered the double doors. A few students milled around.

A girl in glasses turned. "Can we check out books?"

"I don't see why not." I didn't have access to the computer, but I was capable of writing her name and the title of the book down. I eyed the locked drawer. I definitely needed to get it open before they hired a new librarian.

It taunted me in oak laminated finery. I jiggled it for good measure, then headed to the back room. Mrs. Grimes had to have hid the key somewhere in that room. I froze. What if she'd slipped it into her pocket? It would be forever out of my reach.

I could use a little guidance, Lord. I spotted a pair of scissors. There was nothing else to do. I'd have to break the lock. Unless…I picked up the phone. "Cheryl, there's a locked drawer in the library that has something I need and since I don't have keys of my own, do you have extra ones?" I should have done this days ago.

"Of course we do. I'll send a student down with it."

I was such a dunce. The next few minutes were busy checking out books as I watched the clock tick. Mom was going to be upset if I was too late. She'd told me that morning that she had plans to have lunch with Leroy.

"Here's the key." A sour-faced young man dropped a small gold key on the desk.

"Thank you." I opened the drawer, grabbed the papers inside, and dashed back to the front office to sign out. I'd just make it to work on time.

When I arrived at Country Gifts from Heaven, Mom waited by the door, purse in hand. "Talk about cutting it close," she said. "I'll be back in an hour. There's a list of phone numbers by the phone, along with samples, of folks interested in the consignment."

"Thanks." After stashing my purse under the counter, I dug through the samples. There were a few of a good enough quality to add to our shelves. How did I let the other eager crafters down? Maybe, as long as we had the shelf space, I could put out even the bubblegum pink pot holders with missing stitches. If they didn't sell, the crafter might get the idea and give up. It wasn't my place to discourage anyone.

I held up some baby items. These would sell well. Mom and I had discussed carrying baby clothes but neither of us had the time to crochet or sew them. The satin christening gown was especially beautiful with its lace cuffs and shiny ribbon. I smiled, remembering the frilly white gown Lindsey had worn at her baby dedication. Maybe I was a little more open to giving Duane a child of his own than I'd thought.

A dark-colored car pulled in front of the shop. Was it the one idling on the street last night? I narrowed my eyes. I wasn't much for make and model, but I was getting the feeling someone was stalking me. When I moved to open the front door, the car backed up and drove away, but not before I caught a glimpse of baby blue paint on the bumper. With heavily tinted windows, I couldn't make out who drove.

Goose pimples danced up and down my arms. I'd almost come face-to-face with the person responsible for driving Mom and I off the road. It was time to get my pink gun off the closet shelf.

My nerves has settled by the time I called all the numbers on the list Mom had left, letting each of the crafters know to come into the store and sign an agreement giving Country Gifts twenty percent of the proceeds. I spent the next hour clearing a corner of one of the shelves so we could display the products. I'd have Lindsey make up a cute sign when she got out of school. The girl was a whiz at Photoshop.

While I worked, my mind wandered to the papers I'd grabbed from Mrs. Grimes's locked drawer. I itched to take them out and see what was so important, but knew Mom would throw a fit if I didn't wait for her. I watched the clock. She was already ten minutes late. Didn't she know the torture I was going through?

Her white monster of a Caddy pulled into the front parking space. Since she didn't park in the alley, she must not plan on working all day. I met her at the door. "What took you so long? I have some papers for us to look over. Hopefully, they'll give us a clue as to who killed Mrs. Grimes."

"Why didn't you say so earlier? I wouldn't have had pie." She bustled past me.

"I also spotted the car that I think ran us off the road. It parked in the very spot you're in now."

Mom sighed. "All the exciting things happen when you're alone."

Not really, especially considering she was with me when we crashed into the tree. I grabbed my purse and pulled out the papers. The first was an invoice for text books. I'd have to return that to the school. Another one listed what I thought was Mrs. Grimes's antique books. The last sheet, yellowed and tattered around the edges took my breath away.

In my hand I held a treasure map.

8

After a sleepless night dwelling on whether I was in possession of a real treasure map or not, I rolled out of bed to prepare for Mrs. Grimes's memorial. I glanced at the map on my dresser. It certainly looked old enough to be authentic, but who had treasure maps nowadays? Mom had squealed like a little girl at Christmas, saying we'd found the motive for murder.

Had we? Possibly. If the map was real, or someone at least thought it was, treasure was a big motivation. The first mystery I'd gotten involved in had been because of money...the second a misguided attempt at revenge.

I grabbed a few M&Ms from the bag next to the ancient page and shuffled to the bathroom, tossing one of the candies to Cleo who lay with her beautiful head on her paws. She caught the blue disc in midair.

I turned on the shower and sat on the closed toilet lid. My mind wouldn't turn from the fact Mrs. Grimes had flapped her lips about a treasure and someone had killed her for it. Hopefully, a suspect would present themselves at the memorial. At that moment, I had too many suspects to list: the book club, the PTSO, the high school staff, the students. My head ached.

Why did I find myself dragged into these things? I tested the shower spray. Not hot enough. It wasn't like I enjoyed being shot at or taken hostage. It also wasn't always just myself in danger. A few days ago, Mom could have been killed.

My throat seized. What if I turned the map over to Bruce? What if I did and the killer didn't know I did? It wasn't as if I could put a notice in the paper. I'd visit the police station at the first opportunity and present Bruce with a hypothetical situation.

Relieved I had a course of action, I shed my nightclothes and stepped into the shower, letting the water and soap suds wash away my indecision. Once I'd finished and dried off, I padded to my closet. River Valley was small town Southern. No one showed up in anything but a dark-colored dress. I didn't have one.

I poked my head into the hall knowing I would regret what I was being forced to do. "Mom?"

"Why aren't you dressed?" She marched toward me wearing a black long sleeved shirt over a black and white skirt.

"I don't have anything to wear."

"Nonsense." She pushed past me.

I gripped the slipping towel tighter around me while she rummaged through my closet.

"Why are all your clothes so festive? Every woman needs a black dress for funerals and a fancier black dress for nice occasions." She turned, planting her hands on her hips. "You'll have to wear my navy blue dress."

"The sailor one?" Gag. If a strong wind blew, the massive collar would serve as wings.

"Any other ideas?"

"Let me wear what you're wearing."

"Nope. It's the only black I have that is in style. I'll be right back."

I plopped on the edge of my bed and ran my bare foot across Cleo's back. I could not wear the navy dress. I leaped to my feet. I had a peasant skirt with black in it. Sure, it had turquoise and yellow, too, but if I topped it with a black sweater... I dressed as fast as possible, and then slipped my feet into black pumps when I heard Mom thundering down the hall.

"You cannot wear that! We are not going to see a Mariachi band."

"It's not a Mexican skirt. It's peasant." I lifted my hair off my neck and secured it with a black clip.

Mom tossed the sailor dress on the bed. "It's not my fault if people talk about you." She whirled and left.

I eyed the dress with distaste. I'd rather be ridiculed by the women who called themselves River Valley's fashion police. They were all lucky I wasn't wearing my overalls with a black tee-shirt. Up until a few months ago, I lived in those things. Until I bought new clothes and saw the appreciation in Duane's eyes when he saw me dressed as a woman instead of a teenage boy.

As I rushed to the kitchen for toast and coffee, I

passed Lindsey barreling down the hall. "You're late," I called after her.

"I know!" She dashed out and slammed the front door.

My fault, most likely. For the life of me I couldn't get that girl to take responsibility for her own alarm clock. Who set the time for a memorial at eight o'clock in the morning anyway?

Mom and Leroy were sitting at the table, coffee mugs in hand. Mom slid a third one across the table in my direction, then a plate with two slices of toast. "I still think you're dressed wrong."

Leroy eyed me. "She looks fine to me."

"What do you know? You're a man." Mom shook her head.

I took my seat and listened to their good natured bickering. Not being a morning person, I doubted Duane and I would joke first thing in the morning. Poor man. He had no idea what he was getting himself into.

"Time to go." Mom dumped my unfinished coffee.

I held the last piece of toast to my chest unless she got the bright idea of tossing that too, and followed her outside. She slid behind the wheel of the Caddy and glared at me as if daring me to say she couldn't drive. I sighed and climbed in the passenger side. I knew a losing battle when I saw one.

Mrs. Grimes's memorial was held across town at Rivery Valley Funeral Home. From the lack of cars in the parking lot, attendance would be slim. How sad. When I died, I wanted the place standing room only.

The closing of the Cadillac doors echoed across the parking lot. Soft strains of a hymn carried through hidden speakers. Mom and I remained silent as we entered the building and signed the guest book. Five names above ours. Only five people who cared enough about a crotchety old lady to come and say goodbye.

Our feet sank in a carpet plush enough to erase all sound of footsteps. Two flower arrangements stood on each end of the casket. One large, one small. "This is so sad. There's nobody here," I said as we sat in the second row. "We should have brought flowers."

"People are at work. When you have a memorial service in the middle of the day, folks can't take off. You're right. This room should be smelling of too many roses and lillies."

I disagreed. If you cared, you made the time. I settled against the padded back of the pew and watched as the few mourners passed the coffin. Norma Rae and Ingrid Jennings, Cheryl, Estelle Willis, and Mr. Dean. I sniffed and dug for a Kleenex in my purse. I vowed then and there I would find out who killed Mrs. Grimes and why. At least justice could be served for a lonely old woman.

A flashbulb went off and I turned to see Stacy and her ever-present photographer. Why in the world would they be taking pictures? I shoved to my feet. "What are you doing?"

"This is news." Stacy shrugged and leaned closer. "They say the killer always attends the funeral."

"Really? Hard to hide with this many people." I waved my arm. "Have some respect." I'd heard the saying, too, but didn't think it applied to this case.

Bruce entered and stood with arms crossed right inside the door. Obviously, he followed the same theory. I approached him. "Any suspects?"

"Everyone's a suspect." He narrowed his eyes. "You're a suspect."

"Me?" Seriously?

"You were the last one to see her alive." The corner of his mouth twitched. "But, I seriously doubt you're the killer. You have a hard enough time staying alive. No time left to off someone."

"Very funny, Barnie Fife."

"I told you not to call me that."

I rolled my eyes. Police officer or not, I'd known the little weasel too long to take him seriously. Especially after the way he tormented me all through school. "Where's your sidekick?"

"Officer Bradford stayed at the station. There's no need for both of us to be here."

"Did Mrs. Grimes have any family?"

"Nope. She has a cat." He raised his eyebrows. "Want it?"

"No." Lindsey's monster cat Samson would not like a friend. He barely tolerated my German Shepherd, Cleopatra.

"The pound it is. A neighbor has been caring for the mangy thing for the last week and says she detests all the hair."

That was it. I needed to get into Mrs. Grimes's house. There was bound to be a clue. I didn't know where the librarian had lived, but it should be easy enough to find out.

The funeral director took his position behind a simple oak podium, and I hurried back to my seat. He mumbled something about the mark everyone leaves during their time on earth, said a quick prayer, and announced the service was over. There would be no graveside service. Mrs. Grimes would be cremated. I had no idea what they would do with her ashes, only that I definitely didn't want them or her cat.

"Well, that's that." Mom slung her purse over her shoulder. "Time to open the store."

I could work on assigning book fair tasks while waiting the counter. I'd been relieved from the moment the book fair turned from only a haunted house theme to a family affair. With Halloween our least celebrated day of the year, I was most likely the least qualified for that type of attraction. Thank goodness I had enough help, but still, if I didn't learn to multi-task, and fast, I'd be drowning real quick.

I glanced at the coffin. "Wait." I dragged my feet as I approached the maple box. Mrs. Grimes looked almost pleasant with her makeup. Someone had chosen a peacock blue ruffled blouse for her to wear. Her neighbor, maybe?

Around her neck lay a locket. After a quick glance around to make sure no one was watching, I opened the locket. Inside was a younger prettier Mrs. Grimes and a handsome young man. Who was he? He looked familiar. A long lost love? Someone who would mourn her passing? I waved Mom over.

"What?"

"Do you know this man?"

"Are you stealing a dead woman's jewelry?"

I frowned. "Of course not. I'm snooping."

"That's Mr. Dean when he was a young man. They used to date, I think."

I glanced back at the stony look of the high school principal. He didn't look like a grief stricken lover to me. "Should we give him this?"

"He's seen it. If he wanted it, he would have taken it." Mom grabbed my arm. "Let's go before we're kicked out."

I closed the locket and followed Mom, staring at Mr. Dean as I passed. "Check out the locket Mrs. Grimes is wearing," I whispered to Bruce as I passed.

Mr. Dean had just moved to the top of my suspect list.

I stared out the window as Mom drove us to work. I'd call Lynn as soon as possible and leave a message on her phone to call me. Maybe the romance between school principal and librarian hadn't faded over time. Maybe there were rumors floating around the school and Mr. Dean killed the woman who jilted him. It was possible. He could have killed Mrs. Grimes the moment he hired his new Barbie doll of an assistant principal.

My mind whirled with the list of possible motives. Of course, I couldn't discount the treasure map. What if Mrs. Grimes had shared her find during a moment of pillow talk? I shuddered at the mental image.

Of course, I could be wrong and Mr. Dean

completely innocent of murder. Only more time spent investigating would tell.

I glanced up to see Bruce watching us from the funeral home door. I'd have to be careful. He would slap handcuffs on me at the slightest provocation.

9

With an onrush of customers wanting Autumn themed crafts, I couldn't find time to visit Bruce until Thursday. Now, I sat in my rental car and stared at the front door of the police station. I was going to talk hypothetically, but he'd see right through my ruse. Oh, well. Better to just get it over with.

I exited the Mustang and marched through the double glass doors. I stopped at the receptionist desk, surprised to see Ingrid Jennings. I'd assumed she worked at her mother's tea shop.

The plain woman peered at me over her glasses. "May I help you?"

"Hello, Ingrid. I need to see Bruce."

"Do you have an appointment?" She glared at me as if we hadn't met.

"I don't usually need one." Ingrid's unpainted lips thinned. "I'll check to see if he's available, but next time you'll need an appointment. No exceptions." She punched a number into her desk phone and stated that I was here to see him.

Yes, Miss Congeniality. I tapped my foot while I waited.

She hung up the phone. "Go on back."

"Thank you." Golly gee whiz, she was a regular chatty Kathy. I gave her a huge grin and pushed through the waist-high saloon doors to head to Bruce's office. He really needed an office that wasn't behind the receptionist desk. I hated walking through the bull pen. Officer Bradford may not know me well, but Oscar Wilson did.

"In trouble again, Marsha?" He cackled like an old hen.

"Not yet, Oscar."

"Thanks for what you do. The trouble you created the last few months got me stationed back in my hometown. For that, I am eternally grateful."

I sighed and knocked on Bruce's door, then walked in without waiting for him to issue an invitation. "I have a question for you."

"Good morning to you, too." He leaned back in his chair and crossed his arms over his bony chest.

"Sorry, but I need to get to work." I settled into a brown vinyl chair across from him. "If you were to find a treasure map, would you think it was the real thing? Maybe enough of a motive to kill someone?"

"What are you talking about?" He leaned his arms on his desk. "Did you find a treasure map?"

"This is hypothetical."

"Do you have evidence in the murder of Mrs. Grimes? Because if you do –"

"I know, I'd have to turn it in. Can you answer the question?" The man was like a little terrier clinging to my pants leg.

"If treasure maps were real, some fool would probably kill for it, yeah."

"What about a stack of antique books?"

"My God in Heaven you're trying to solve Mrs. Grimes's murder." He shoved back his chair. It slammed into the wall behind him. "Lord, save us all from Marsha Steele. I can't keep saving you. One of these days, I'll be too late."

Puh-leeze. "Save me? Excuse me, but I've managed to get out of every scrape myself." Mostly. He did come running with Duane when a mad woman and her son held me at gunpoint, but by then, I had the two crazy people yelling at each other instead of aiming the gun at me. The first crime I'd solved, I tazed the woman and got away. By myself. All Bruce did was lock them up after I was done with them.

"If you get in the way of my investigation," Bruce said. "I will arrest you. Give me this so-called treasure map."

Sure, right after I make a photocopy. "Don't worry. I won't get in your way." I stood.

"Famous last words. I have a holding cell with your name on it."

"I hope it's decorated nicely." Tossing him my best smile, I turned and left his office. Next on my agenda, find out where Mrs. Grimes lived. Mom would know.

Back at the store, I waited while Mom rang up a customer buying several quilt books and yards of fabric. Next to her sat a pile from our scrap bin. I wished Mom wouldn't give those away. We could package and sell them. When had I gotten so money hungry? When I'd become a single mother with a wedding to pay for.

Once the customer left, I grabbed a soda from the fridge and a granola bar to carry in my purse for later. "Mom, where did Mrs. Grimes live?"

"On Elm Street." She wiped loose threads from the counter into her hand. "The mailbox looks like a stack of books. Why?"

I'd seen that house before. "I'm going snooping."

Mom whirled, dropping the threads onto the floor. "I want to go."

"Who is going to keep the shop open?"

"Why should you have all the fun? We'll go on our lunch hour."

We never took a lunch hour, staggering our lunches instead to keep the store open. "We'll be trespassing. Bruce has already threatened to arrest me."

"He wouldn't dare. Not while I'm with you. Why, I knew his mother." Her face lit with expectation. "Let me grab my camera, and we'll leave right away."

I sighed and jotted a quick note on a sheet of paper that we'd be back at eleven. An early lunch, I guess. "I'm driving this time. My rental is less conspicuous." I really needed to start shopping for a new car.

"It's red." Mom shook her head and dashed out the backdoor toward her white beast.

She could sit out there until doomsday. I was driving this time. I headed out the front door and waited behind the wheel of my car.

Two minutes later, Mom parked the Caddy right behind me, blocking me in. She honked.

"I said I'm driving," I yelled out my window.

She honked again. "Try getting around me."

"Fine." I started the ignition, then pulled forward a couple of inches, then back, then forward, turning my wheel.

"Don't you hit my car," she called out.

"Then move!" I kept maneuvering until I found myself diagonal and thoroughly wedged between our shop and the dentist next door. "You win. Move so I can straighten out, then I'll join you." As if. The moment she moved her boat of a car, I sped down Main Street toward Elm, leaving Mom to follow. We were about as inconspicuous as two purple elephants blowing trumpets.

I parked around the corner from Mrs. Grimes's house. Mom pulled in behind me. "That was dirty pool," she said marching past me.

"You asked for it." I jogged beside her. "We need to have a story to tell if someone asks why we're here."

"We'll think of something." Mom set her chin, clearly put off by my shenanigans. She marched up to the front door and knocked.

Mrs. Grimes's house was painted a cheery yellow with a bright red front door. White lace curtains hung at the spotless windows. Flower boxes, full of autumn mums, hung under both front windows. The house resembled a storybook cottage.

"Nobody's home," Mom said.

"Of course not, she's deceased." I cupped my

hands around my eyes and peered in the window beside the door. "We'll have to get in another way."

"Let's try the back." Mom led the way to a small door off the kitchen. It was locked. "Maybe we can pick the lock. This is an old house." She pulled a packet of sharp objects from her purse. "I bought these lock picks off eBay and watched a YouTube video on how to use them. I thought they might come in handy with crime solving."

We were going to be arrested for sure. "Who are you and what have you done with my mother?"

"Oh, hush. I'm trying to concentrate." She bent over and got to work while I kept a sharp eye out for any curious onlookers.

A loud click and she swung the door open. "Voila." She grinned over her shoulder. "Am I amazing or what?"

"Hurry and get inside before someone sees us." I shoved against her back.

We stepped into a cheery yellow kitchen with painted metal cabinets and modern appliances. "Look for anything that might tell us why she was killed."

"Put these on." Mom handed me a pair of rubber gloves.

"You scare me." I donned the gloves and headed for the back of the house, leaving Mom to do the front.

Off the hall, I found two bedrooms and a bathroom. Only one bedroom looked as if anyone lived in it, so I chose to check that one. The other room looked like a guestroom slash office.

I opened the closet. A line of dresses hung from

the rod. Shoe boxes lined the shelf. Labels signified what was in each of them. Some were shoes, one was receipts, and one said important papers. I stretched my short frame to pull it down. Something rubbed against my ankles. I screamed and fell backward, banging my hip on the dresser. At my feet sat a beautiful silver Persian cat with yellow eyes. "Well, hello, gorgeous. I thought the neighbor was keeping you?"

Had the poor thing been alone all this time? He must be starving.

"What's wrong? What did you find?" Mom burst into the room. "Oh, isn't he lovely?"

"Bruce asked me if I wanted Mrs. Grimes's cat, but when I said no, he told me the neighbor would take it to the pound. I guess that isn't true. I hope he hasn't been locked up in here alone all week."

"You'll have to take him, Marsha. You can't let this beautiful animal be euthanized."

"You take him. Samson won't be happy." I reached again for the box. Getting a hold of it, I set it on the bed.

"I am so good at this. Really, I've missed my calling." Mom pulled a rose-colored book from the nightstand. "Here is Harriet's journal."

The doorbell rang. Mom shoved the journal under her shirt. I shoved the box of papers back in the closet and pulled off my gloves. "The gloves," I hissed. Scooping the cat into my arms, I headed for the front door. A peek outside sent my heart plummeting to my toes.

Bruce peered through the keyhole.

I took a deep breath and opened the door.

"Hello, Bruce, what brings you here?"

"A neighbor called about suspicious characters in a dead woman's house. Why are you here?"

I held up the cat. "You did tell me to take him, did you not?"

"You said no."

"I had second thoughts."

"How did you know he would still be here?" He stepped past me into the house. "Mrs. Bohan, I'm surprised to see you."

Mom crossed her arms. "Don't start with me young man. I knew your mother."

He opened and closed his mouth a few times, then shook his head. "How did you get in?"

"The back door was open," I said. Well, it was by the time I entered. "We'll take this sweetie and go now, shall we?" I motioned my head toward the front door.

"I'll just get my purse off the counter." Mom skedaddled to the kitchen, tossed her little leather pack into her purse, while holding a hand to her side to keep the journal in place, then dashed back to me.

"Why are you holding your side?" Bruce asked.

"Oh, it's nothing, really." Mom widened her eyes. Instead of the innocent look she was most likely trying for, she looked deranged. "The cat startled me, and I bumped into the counter. See you later." She grabbed my arm with an iron grip and dragged me from the house.

"We need to get to the cars," she said. "Before Bruce wonders why we didn't park in the driveway like normal people."

We were far from normal. I glanced back.

Bruce stood on the porch and watched us scurry away like the guilty people we were.

10

With working at the shop and meetings for the book fair, Marsha had yet to dig into Mrs. Grimes's journal. Now, it was Saturday and the day Lynn was picking her up to go dress shopping. "Lindsey, she'll be here any minute! Mom?"

"Settle down," Mom called from the kitchen. "We're ready."

Marsha stormed into the kitchen and reached over the refrigerator for her M&Ms. The day called for her stress reliever and a venti-sized coffee at the coffee shop. Her first wedding had been a quick, thrown together affair when Marsha had donned her mother's old wedding dress. Now, she was shopping for a new one and had no idea what she was looking for. Should she even wear white? As a widowed mother, maybe she should be happy with a sundress.

"Why aren't you smiling?" Mom handed me a cup of coffee. "This is a fun day. We closed the shop for the occasion."

"I don't think I need a wedding dress. I can go to the department store and buy a pretty sundress

I'll wear again."

"Mom!" Lindsey pouted. "I'm looking forward to this. I want a gorgeous bridesmaid dress so I'll look awesome in the pictures."

"Fine, but why do I have to wear a big frilly gown?"

"They aren't all frilly," Lynn said strolling into the kitchen. "I hope you don't mind me just barging in. The front door was unlocked. Not wise, considering Marsha is neck deep in murder again. Oh, pretty." She petted Prince, Mrs. Grimes's cat, who would not stay off the counters no matter how many times we rattled a can of marbles or sprayed him with water.

Maybe it had something to do with the German Shepherd staring up at him and licking her lips. Or the fact that Samson the monster cat hissed everything the fancy cat came near him.

"Mom doesn't want to buy a wedding dress," Lindsey said. "I think she thinks she's too old or something."

"I never said that." I grabbed another handful of candy. "I'm a widowed mother. This isn't my first marriage."

"Nobody cares about that anymore. Buy the wedding dress of your dreams. Oh." Lynn popped out and returned moments later with four mocha flavored blended coffees. "I set these on the foyer table to close the door and left them. Are we ready to go?"

I sighed. "As ready as I'll ever be." I wanted to marry Duane with all my heart, but the planning that went along with it gave me hives. I wasn't the type to want to be the center of attention.

We trooped out to Lynn's modest Toyota Corolla. Mom and Lindsey climbed in the back, leaving the shotgun seat to me. I sipped my frozen drink and stared out the window. I knew without asking that Lynn would take me to the ritziest wedding shop around. She didn't disappoint. Thirty minutes later we parked in front of an old Victorian house turned wedding dress venue. I took a deep breath and slid out of the car.

"Don't worry," Lynn said. "Leave this to me. We'll have you looking beautiful."

We trooped inside to be greeted by a lovely, friendly woman with fake boobs and a genuine smile. "Welcome to Monique's. Which one is the bride?"

I raised my hand and forced a smile.

"Lovely. What type of gown are you looking for?"

I glanced in desperation at my maid-of-honor. Lynn grinned. "Something in off-white, not too fancy, very classy in the price range of twelve hundred dollars. We are also looking for a mother-of-the bride dress, which we hope to get for free by also purchasing two bridesmaids gowns."

My best friend the negotiator.

"I'm sure we can work something out." The saleslady, her nametag labeled her as Veronica, tapped a manicured finger to her lips. "As long as we keep the bridesmaid dresses and mother's dress in the two hundred dollar range?"

"Perfect." Lynn followed her as if Lynn were the bride to be instead of me.

As we passed row after row of dresses, I began to hyperventilate. How did anyone make a decision with so many choices?

Veronica led us to a round platform of mirrors and pulled back a curtain. "This is where you will change and observe your choices. Have a seat, grab a bottle of water, and I'll be back with some gowns for you to look at."

I'd rather stare down the barrel of a gun. Seeing as that wasn't an option at the moment, I stepped onto a small platform and studied my petite figure. I'd lost weight in the last few months, no longer looking like a matron. Instead, a trim thirty-six year old with crazy auburn hair stared back at me. Maybe I could pull this off after all. "I don't want a veil. A headband will do just fine."

"That should be cute," Lynn said.

"What will Duane lift when he kisses you?" Mom plopped onto a plush divan.

"We've already kissed, Mom. Several times." I turned and studied my rear end. Still curvy, but the right dress should make me look flatter.

"I'm going to glance at the rack of bridesmaid dresses." Lindsey disappeared around the corner.

"Okay," Mom said. "But there's something romantic about a veil."

Veronica returned with five dresses. The first one I tried on was a vintage style with delicate lace covering the entire satin underdress. I closed the curtain and changed. The dress fit me like a glove. I felt like a princess. Tears welled in my eyes and I tossed back the curtain.

Mom gasped, putting a hand to her mouth. Lynn

clapped. Lindsey froze, several gowns in different colors in her arms. "I've never seen you so pretty," she said.

"This is the one I want." I turned in a slow circle. The sleeves of the gown sat just off my shoulders. The neck dipped to a V hinting at cleavage but stopping short of actually showing any. The train swept two feet behind me.

"Try on the others first," Lynn said. "But that one is gorgeous." She peeked at the price tag. "Twelve hundred and fifty dollars. Perfect."

I tried on a dress that skimmed my hips and trailed onto the floor in a cathedral style train, then one that was all smooth, but swished around my ankles. Disregarding the last two, I tried back on the first one, running my hands over hips as soft as a baby's bottom. I was in love and finally knew why women put so much effort into finding the perfect dress for their wedding. I didn't want to take it off.

"Our turn, Mom." Lindsey hung up a rainbow of dresses. "I think the muted rose color will go with your old-fashioned gown."

I agreed, but didn't like her description of my "precious". The dress was my "ring" from the Lord of the Rings trilogy, and I didn't want to let it go.

"Once you pick the style you like," Veronica said. "We can have them made in any color you choose."

They decided on simple off-the-shoulder gowns that fell to the knees with a sash in a slightly darker shade than the dress. I was getting my wish, simple but elegant. Nothing too frilly. Even Mom didn't disappoint. She chose a simple sheath dress in a mango color with a small matching jacket.

"Now, all we need is to find the perfect shoes." Lynn drew in a deep breath. "But lunch first."

"Let's go to the tea shop on Main Street." I might as well get in a little sleuthing.

The others were in agreement. After putting a deposit on the gowns, we headed back to River Valley and stepped into an overly decorated front room of yet another renovated Victorian. Norma Rae greeted us, dressed in vintage clothing to fit the era. She led us to a small round table in an alcove. Other than one other woman, we were the only customers. Probably because we had to slide into our seats sideways because of all the decorations surrounding the tables. Folks wanted to eat with elbow room, not have to worry about knocking a knickknack onto the floor.

"Ask her if business is okay." I elbowed Mom when Norma Rae left to fetch tea and sandwiches.

"It's none of my business."

"Like that's ever stopped you before. Do it. We're trying to establish our suspect list." Since Norma Rae knew Mrs. Grimes very well, it stood to reason that the woman might also know about the treasure map.

Norma Rae returned several minutes later with Turkey and white cheddar sandwiches and pomegranate tea. "Enjoy."

"Dear," Mom glanced around the room. "This is such a darling place. How's business?"

"It could definitely be better." Norma Rae's chin quivered. "I'm in danger of losing my home to be honest with you. I live upstairs. Not to mention that Ingrid may have to move in with me if she doesn't find a way to pay off her mound of debt. I love my daughter, but can't abide the thought of sharing my small space with her. Oh, why am I burdening you with my troubles?" She straightened and glanced at each of us. "It's my business. I've something in the works that will take care of everything. Let me know if I can serve you further." She whirled and stepped through a curtained door.

Well, the woman definitely seemed to need a chunk of money. Thus, a motive for murder under the right circumstances. I sipped the fragrant tea. Quite good.

"Are you happy?" Mom wiped her mouth with an embroidered napkin. "We've probably ruined that poor woman's day by reminding her of her problems."

"We could always give her suggestions for running a successful business, but I doubt she'd listen." I picked up my sandwich and dwelled on what type of shoes I might want to go with the dress. Maybe a champagne colored pair of sandals with a kitten heel?

"I'm going to offer anyway," Mom said. "It's the least we can do. You know how I like to help those in need."

"If she says yes, you can prod her for more information."

Lynn sighed. "Can't we have an outing without gathering clues? I'm sure Lindsey isn't interested."

"Yes, I am," Lindsey said. "We're the three Callahans, a crime-solving group of three generations." She lifted her tea cup in a toast.

"Mom and Grandma may no longer be Callahans, but that stubborn blood runs in all of our veins."

"Isn't that the truth." Lynn shook her head. "Fine. What do you want me to do? I might as well get in on the fun. I've managed to stay out of it for months."

"Seriously?" I straightened, not believing my good fortune. "Can you ask around the school to see whether anyone held a grudge against Mrs. Grimes? Subtly, of course."

"Of course." She set her cup on its saucer. "I can tell you right now the woman wasn't very liked by anyone, except for maybe Cheryl. She likes everyone, but I can bring up the murder during prep and lunch time and see what others say."

I reached across the table and grabbed her hand. "You're the best friend ever."

"Don't you forget it, either." She returned the squeeze. "Just don't get me held at gunpoint, okay? I'll freak out."

"I'll do my best, but no promises."

"I need some gum." Lindsey grabbed my purse and opened it. "Mom, why do you have a gun in here?"

"Shhh." I grabbed my purse. "Don't announce it to the world!"

"You think someone is going to try to kill you again, don't you?" Tears welled in my daughter's eyes. "I'd kind of like my children to have a grandmother."

"Oh, sweetie. I'm perfectly safe this time."

"What about that car running us off the road?" Mom raised her eyebrows.

"You told me you slid in a puddle of water." Lindsey tossed down her napkin. "Can't you snoop without making people mad at you?" She stood and marched toward a door that said restroom.

The rest of us watched her go. I shrugged. "You can't solve a murder without danger."

11

Sunday afternoon, I took a break between church and supper to finally dig through Mrs. Grimes's journal. Her penmanship looked like a typewriter font. Her entries were about Sir Galahad, the cat, mostly. Sometimes she mentioned frustrations with the "insipid fools" from the book club. Way to win friends and influence people, Mrs. Grimes.

Another entry mentioned a deep burning desire to quit her job at the school and run off to Mexico with the man of her dreams. Surely she didn't mean Mr. Dean. I gagged. Reading someone else's private thoughts was both entertaining and embarrassing, yet I couldn't stop. When I reached a particularly intimate moment with her boy toy, yes, she actually called him those words, I skipped to the last few pages of the book.

Bingo! Mrs. Grimes saw the fulfillment of everything she'd dreamed of in the form of an old pirate's treasure map stuck between the pages of a book. While the book itself wasn't worth a lot of money, she trusted the map to be real and was searching for someone knowledgeable about old maps.

I closed the journal and stared out my bedroom window. I'd have to give Bruce a copy of the journal and the map. Once he found out I'd taken something from the victim's home, he'd arrest me for sure. I never should have told him about the map. I could mail the journal anonymously, but he already knew I had the map in my possession. Or, I could just put the journal back into her house. That would definitely impede the investigation, though. I couldn't do it. I'd have to take my chances and pay him another visit. Two hours in the dental chair sounded like more fun.

Grabbing my purse from the dresser, I checked my hair, then shuffled out the door, sure I'd be spending the night in jail, or at least a few hours until Duane or Mom bailed me out. I couldn't help it. I couldn't keep the journal and map, not when it might provide Bruce with the information he needed to solve the case.

I stopped in the home office long enough to make a copy of the map on our printer. Then, I folded the original, stuck it in the pages of the journal, and headed to my rental car. Bruce wouldn't be working on a Sunday, not with a rookie on the force, so instead of heading to the police station I drove to his modest ranch house on the outskirts of town.

When I pulled into his driveway, Bruce sat on his front porch in basketball shorts and a white tank top. I shook my head to try and rid my mind of his bony legs poking from the bottom of the shorts. At least he wasn't in uniform. It might be easier to hand the things over to him if he looked like a regular citizen. I exited the car, tucked the journal under my arm, and marched toward him.

"It must not be good news if you're coming to my house." Bruce met me at the steps to his porch.

I handed him the journal. "Here is Mrs. Grimes's journal and the treasure map. I hope it helps you find the person who killed her."

His eyebrows lowered. "How did you get this?"

"Mom found it when we went to fetch the cat. His name is Sir Galahad." I straightened my shoulders and put my hands behind my back. Maybe if he didn't see them, he wouldn't be tempted to cuff me.

He sighed. "You read it?"

"Most of it."

"And you feel it contains something of importance?"

Well, duh. "It gives a motive. Mrs. Grimes received the treasure map along with a shipment of antique books. Whether or not the map is real, someone most likely thinks it is."

"Who do you suspect?" Bruce leaned against the railing.

Was he actually asking for my opinion? "I have too many to mention at this time, but rest assured, I have spies digging for information."

"I'm sure you do. You probably also kept a copy of the map, correct?"

"I plead the fifth."

"Does this mean you'll stop sticking your nose where it doesn't belong?"

Right. Dream on. "No, it means I'll share whatever information I find. Have a good day." I flashed him a grin and almost skipped to my car. He hadn't arrested me. I drove on clouds all the way home.

When I went in the house, everyone was in the living room watching the Hogs play football. I perched on the arm of the chair Duane sat in and kissed the top of his head.

He grabbed my hand. "Where were you?"

"Turning evidence over to Bruce."

"Are you feeling sick?" Duane chuckled. "This has got to be a first."

I punched his shoulder. "I always turn things over when I'm finished with them."

"Now we can't find the treasure." Mom handed me a diet soda.

"Oh, I kept a copy of the map."

"Treasure? What treasure?" Leroy perked up. "Let's see that map."

I rushed to the office and grabbed the photocopy, but not before printing off two more copies and slipping them into a file marked bills. "This belonged to Mrs. Grimes. Does it mean anything to you?" I held out the paper as I dashed back into the room.

Leroy studied the map. "This shows the location of all the places Jesse James and his brother stashed their loot. Supposedly, there are four locations in Arkansas. One in Hot Springs, one around Paragould, one in Springdale, and one around Mena. More fools than you'd see at the Macy's Thanksgiving Day parade has looked for these treasures."

"So it isn't real?" I plopped on the sofa.

"The map is real all right." He handed it back to me. "I just doubt whether there's anything there. I'm sure Jesse James's cohorts retrieved this stuff a long time ago. Everyone and their Grandma have gone looking for these treasures."

"But what if?" Lindsey pulled her gaze away from the television. "It could be there or at least one of the places. We could be rich."

"Someone killed for this map," Mom reminded her. "You'll have to stay home when we search."

"That's so unfair!" Lindsey pouted. "I'm not a child, you know."

"No one is going anywhere," Leroy said. "It's a wild goose chase."

What if it wasn't? What if the killer somehow knew the treasure was still there and only needed the map in order to retrieve it. In desperation, they could have threatened Mrs. Grimes and when she didn't cave, they killed her. Some people would do anything for money.

Leroy ripped the map into shreds. "Now, none of you crazy females will go looking for something that will get you killed."

Mom and Lindsey's mouths dropped open. I clamped my mouth closed and did my best to look furious. Good thing I made extra copies. Sometimes, I surprised myself with my intelligence.

I met Mom's gaze. From the determined look in her eyes, we'd be heading to the spots on the map at the first opportunity. From the look on Duane's face, he realized the same thing, and with all four places on the map scattered from one corner of Arkansas to the other, we'd have to find a way to be gone for a few days. Something I couldn't do. Not with organizing the book fair. "There's no way I have time to check this out."

"I'll take you to one on Saturday." Duane pulled me from the sofa and into his arms. "If I don't, you'll drive yourself crazy thinking about it."

"We can make it a family trip." Mom jumped to her feet. "This calls for tea." She raced to the kitchen, leaving the rest of us laughing.

I wrapped my arms around Duane's neck. "Saturday sounds wonderful." I'd have to work overtime on the fair during the week, but it would be worth it if we found something.

"Saturday is our busiest day of the week," Mom said. "But I guess it wouldn't be good to take off church on Sunday to go treasure hunting. I'll put a sign up tomorrow so we give our customers plenty of notice."

"I'll post something on the website, too," Lindsey said. "Regardless of what y'all say, I'm going with you. This is the coolest thing in a long time. We can use grandpa's old metal detector."

I'd forgotten about that old thing. Mom had kept all Dad's things in the guest house, and I'd gone through it all before moving in there until Mom married Leroy and we changed places. I'd put all the keepable things in the back closet. "That's a good idea. Oh, and the wedding colors are ivory and vintage rose."

"Pink?" Duane frowned. "You want me to wear pink?"

I pulled back. "It isn't pink. It's rose."

"Same thing. Can I wear all black?"

I tweaked his nose. "You can wear anything you want." I meant it. He'd be gorgeous in jeans and a tee-shirt. I lowered my voice. "Want to elope?"

"And risk your mother's wrath? I don't think so." He gave me a quick kiss and sat back down to watch the game. I counted myself lucky I was able to drag him away for even a couple of minutes.

I moved to the kitchen and spread out my notes on the book fair. Things were falling into place. Cheryl had emailed me with the list of attractions: face painting, darts, a bounce house, a fish bowl toss, and the final extravaganza was the haunted hall leading to the library. Duane and Leroy would build it, also acting as macabre characters. Lindsey said all her friends were looking forward to it and she hoped it wouldn't be lame. I promised to do my best.

Now the task to make it exciting loomed in front of me. Maybe a horde of zombies that wandered the hall and a chainsaw welding maniac would keep things lively. I'd also need monsters that popped up from hidden places. Maybe an acted out scene or two of some grisly medical procedure that participants would watch. I jotted down my ideas.

Why didn't today's teens enjoy the simple things like three-legged races and ice cream socials? We still had the milder forms of entertainment at church every year and they seemed to enjoy themselves, but Halloween was an entirely different matter. Today's youth wanted to be scared spitless. Maybe a scene of hell and brimstone with a laughing Satan would do the trick. That was certainly enough to scare me.

Having organized my notes, I turned to my list of suspects. Mr. Dean was the only name on the page. I added the members of the book club, having a strong feeling that Mrs. Grimes had blabbed to them about the map. I tapped the ink pen against my front teeth, and then added the small amount of PTSO members. If the librarian was as prolific with her verbal words as she was with the written ones, she'd most likely told anyone close enough to listen that she might soon be in possession of a treasure.

I prayed this mystery wouldn't see another death. The body count on the last two had been several with me almost being one of them. So far, God had kept me and my family safe from my nosiness. How long would that protection last when I actively put myself in harm's way?

The doorbell rang. "I'll get it." I headed to the foyer and opened the front door.

A serious faced Bruce stood on the front porch. "I need to talk to you."

"Okay." I stepped outside and pulled the door closed. "Am I in trouble?"

"I got this taped to my front door. I hope you'll heed the warning." He handed me a slip of yellow computer paper.

"Tell Marsha Steele to stay out of it."

12

The craft group was in full swing making quilts for the nursery of River Valley's homeless shelter. Their laughter and conversation kept me entertained as I refilled the pitcher of sweet tea.

"Marsha knows what I'm talking about," Dottie Baker, the woman I'd saved from a maniac a few months ago said. Bless her heart. She'd been my advocate ever since.

I lifted the tray with the pitcher and small sandwiches and waltzed into the back room. "I know what?" I set the tray on a side counter.

"That people will kill for money." Dottie waved a curved quilting needle in the air. "We know first hand the evil that resides in men, and women. Gertie was telling us about a treasure map you found that belonged to Mildred. It's got to be about money. Half this town wouldn't turn down a fortune."

"I still say that most people are honest and hardworking." Betty Larson, the oldest of the group at eighty, stabbed her needle through the yellow quilt. "I refuse to think otherwise."

"I agree," I said. "But if someone is in dire straits, some will kill. Who in this town needs money in a bad way?"

"Get your notepad, girlie," Dottie said. "And we'll tell you."

"Thank you. You ladies were a great help with the last mystery." I grabbed a notepad from a drawer and sat down.

Mom got up and closed the back door. "No sense in letting anyone within hearing distance get an earful."

She most likely meant Leroy if he wandered by. Poor man. He hadn't gotten used to the idea yet that his new wife was a Jane Marple wanna be. Me, I preferred Nancy Drew.

"Okay." Dottie set down her needle. "First off, there's Norma Rae Jennings. She's about to lose that over-decorated tea shop. If she does, then her mouse of a daughter, Ingrid, will have to live with her. Those two are like a rabbit and a snake, if you get my meaning. Then, there's Brad and Janet Snyder. Everyone knows they're up to their necks in debt because of Brad's gambling habits. Mr. Dean has a secret, but no one here has been able to ferret it out."

She took a dramatic gulp of tea. "Estelle Willis, the English teacher at the high school, hates teaching, or so I've heard. Wants to retire somewhere exotic and write her own murder mystery. Then, there's the school office manager, Sarah Boatwright, who spends money like she's dropping breadcrumbs."

My pen flew across the paper. I knew these ladies wouldn't fail me.

"Don't forget that new cop in town," Betty pointed out. "No one knows anything about him. He's too pretty for his own good. That kind of good looks on a man often hides an evil heart, no offense, Marsha. We all know Duane is the best looking man in town, but he has a heart of gold. Why, if I were thirty years younger—hubba hubba."

"Stop it, you old flirt." Dottie, winner of the last two years beauty pageant at the retirement home, hated anyone to upstage her.

"You pink haired old biddy!" Betty tried pushing back her chair. Her toothpick arms barely budged her.

"I pay a lot of money for this shade. It goes with my porcelain complexion. You're just jealous." Dottie did succeed in getting to her feet.

"You just wait until I get up." Betty's chair moved an inch.

"Ladies." I bit my lip to keep from laughing. "We're on the same side here. If we're going to catch the person who killed Mrs. Grimes, we have to work together."

"Fine." Dottie sat back down. "But I want it on record that I'm working with Betty in protest."

"Me, too!" Betty glowered.

The bell over the front door jingled, releasing me from comic hell. I hurried to wait on the customer. Stacy sashayed into the store. Maybe I'd prefer the old ladies.

"Can I help you?" I pasted on a smile.

"This is the day the women get together and

craft, isn't it?" She held up a shopping bag. "I've come to craft."

"They're working on quilts today."

"Wonderful. I'd like to learn."

Snoop and dig for newsworthy information was more like it. I wasn't worried. The ladies would clam up the moment Stacy strolled in. My heart clenched. I shouldn't act that way. Maybe Stacy was turning over a new leaf and actually wanted to help people. I shot a quick prayer for forgiveness heavenward and followed the sweet perfumed scent trail to the back room.

"This day just keeps getting better." Betty tried getting up again. "Will someone please help me to my feet?"

I rushed to her side. "You aren't leaving, are you?"

"I'm going to powder my nose." She glared at Stacy on her way past.

"What's her beef with you?" I resumed my seat.

Stacy shrugged. "I posted a nice little tidbit about shoplifting in the paper a month ago. Seems our dear Mrs. Larson was supplementing her income by selling stolen goods."

Really? I glanced at the restroom door. You never could tell with some people.

Stacy set out several unopened packages of craft supplies. "What does a person use for quilting?"

"A needle and thread." Mom rolled her eyes and handed Stacy a pieced together pillow top. "You can learn by quilting this. Just sew in the rows."

Stacy grinned. "I can do this. After all, it can't be different than sewing on a button."

Dottie snorted. "Aren't you the clever girl? Do you have a tape recorder in that bag of yours?"

"You wound me, Dottie, you really do." Stacy stuck her tongue out and narrowed her eyes, trying to slip thread through the eye of a needle. "I'm more than a pretty face and a reporter, you know." Her gaze fell on my notes. She made a grab for the paper, but I snatched it up before her fingers grasped hold. "What's that?"

"A shopping list." I ripped off the top page and shoved it in the pocket of my apron. If Stacy got a hold of the list of suspects, the whole town would see it in the morning's paper.

Her face fell. "I don't take everything to the paper. We didn't print about Bruce receiving a warning for you to stay out of this latest investigation. That would endanger your life further, and the paper isn't about that."

The group's voice rose in alarm. I sighed. I'd wanted to keep the threat against me a secret. "How did you find out about that?"

Stacy gave a thin smile. "I have my resources. Why don't you let me help you this time? As a reporter, I have good investigative skills."

She had a good point, but my distrust of her went back to high school when she'd try to steal Duane away from me. Could I let that go and accept the help she was offering?

Everyone remained silent and waited for my answer. I looked around the table at each of their dear faces. I didn't want to draw anyone else into the danger I felt creeping up behind me. Why had I been the one to find Mrs. Grimes? Why had I stepped forward to continue with a book fair that wasn't in a volunteer's job description? Because I felt this overwhelming need to prove myself. Since my first husband's death, I'd strived to be the best at everything: a mother, a daughter, a business owner, and now a solver of crime. Why couldn't I be happy with the things other people were happy with?

Did it have something to do with marrying Robert out of spite because his brother, my true love, had deserted me for bigger things? Did I feel like I needed to be something more in order to keep Duane from leaving again?

"It's dangerous." I'd made my decision. If Stacy wanted to help, she might have resources unavailable to me.

"I'm up to the task." She glanced around the table. "Will y'all have me?"

The women glanced at each other, then as one, they nodded.

"But if we find one thing said in private printed in that paper, you'll have to answer to us," Betty said. "That will not be pleasant for you."

Stacy grinned. "No, I imagine it wouldn't."

I couldn't shake the feeling we'd turned a corner, Stacy and I. A dark corner full of danger and death.

The women cleaned up their supplies and left, chattering like a bunch of teenage girls over the things discussed that morning. Like the crusty dears they were, they included Stacy in their conversation as if she'd always been a part of their clique. My heart swelled. Each and every one of those old ladies held a special place in my heart, even more so after a killer had put a bulls eye on every one of their backs a few months ago.

Through luck, determination, and God's grace, I'd managed to keep them safe. Maybe that was the real reason I put myself in harm's way. To protect the ones I loved from being taken from me before their time.

I folded the quilt top and placed it safely on a shelf until next week. I wasn't sure what Stacy intended to do, since we'd accepted her but not filled her in on our suspects. If she didn't know who we were watching, how could she investigate? I glanced at my watch. Lunch time. "Mom, I'm heading to the coffee shop for a sandwich. Do you want anything?"

"Yeah, one of them Panini things and some mango tea." She carried the snack tray to the sink. "When you get back, we'll come up with a game plan to check out everyone on that list."

Good ole' Mom. Always thinking. I slung my purse over my shoulder and dashed across the street.

A dark sedan roared toward me. I leaped onto the sidewalk. As the car sped past, I spotted a swath of baby blue paint across the fender. That was the car that had run me and Mom off the road.

Instead of entering the coffee shop, I sprinted down the sidewalk, dodging window shoppers. The car stopped at the red light. My lungs burned. I had to get close enough to see through the tinted windows. If I could catch a glimpse of the driver, I'd know who the killer was.

The light turned green and the car moved down Main Street. The knowledge I might be close to knowing the killer's identity spurred me on. I leaped over the leash of a dog tied to a fire hydrant and tried to ignore my gasping breath. I really needed to get in better shape.

The car slowed and turned the corner. I took a short cut through the alley. Chasing a possible murderer might not be the smartest thing I'd ever done, but I didn't stop to put much thought in my actions. I kept my eyes and mind on the goal. The car passed the entrance to the alley.

The whoop of a siren sounded as I burst from the alley. I swerved to avoid running into Bruce's squad car. The slam of a door told me he was following. Wonderful. Someone called the police about a suspicious character running the streets.

"Stop!" Bruce called.

Since he didn't add "or I'll shoot" I kept running. His footsteps pounded behind me.

I tripped over a tree root and went sprawling on my hands. Concrete scraped the skin from my palms. I rolled over to my back and glared at my pursuer. "Catch that car. It's the killer."

He took one look at me and dashed away. Thank goodness, for once in his life, he didn't stop to ask a lot of questions.

I got to my feet and wiped my bloody hands on my thighs. I was going to throttle Bruce when he came back, which unfortunately was seconds later.

"Dogs chase cars, Marsha," he said.

"I almost had the killer."

"What would you have done with them once

you caught them?" He glared.
"Shoot them."

13

Bruce didn't have to look so shocked. I wouldn't really have shot them.

I limped down the sidewalk to the coffee shop and headed to the restroom in back. After washing the blood from my hands and skinned knees, I was more ready for caffeine than before. A chocolate java might ease the pain of the knees being ripped out of my new jeans. My raw hands burned.

"Hey, Marsha."

I turned to see Officer Wilson at a corner table. "Officer Wilson. It's good to see you."

He stood and wound through the tables to my side. "I heard you're looking for a new car."

"Yes, sir." I slid a twenty-dollar bill across the counter. "Something with good gas mileage."

"I've got a little jeep that used to belong to my brother. It's a ninety-five but has a new engine and it's been well cared for. You can have it for five thousand."

"Really?" That would leave money left over after the insurance settlement that I could spend on the wedding. "When can I look at it?"

His gaze landed on my ripped jeans and skinned

knees. "Maybe you should go home and change first." He jotted his address down on the back of his business card. "I'm home all day."

"Thanks." I grabbed the carrier with mine and mom's lunches then headed back across the street to the store.

"What the heck happened to you?" Mom paused in her sweeping. "You were gone too long for merely going across the street."

I set the carrier on the counter. "The car that ran us off the road almost hit me when I was crossing the street. I ran after it, but Bruce got in the way so the car drove off." I wrapped my hands around my cup, the cold of the blended drink soothing my torn skin. "Then, I saw Officer Wilson in the coffee shop, and he said he has a jeep I can look at later."

"You need a race car so you can outrun the fool in the sedan." Mom propped the broom against the wall and reached for her sandwich. "Does the jeep have four wheel drive?"

"I don't know, why?"

"Because then if someone wants to run you off the road, you can actually go off the road."

I shook my head at her logic. The last thing I wanted was another face-to-face meeting with a tree. My knees screamed as I lowered myself in a chair. Duane was going to have a fit when he got a look at me. The knees I could hide—the hands, not so much. It wasn't near cold enough outside for gloves.

The phone on the counter rang. I reached for the receiver and brought it to my ear. "Country Gifts from Heaven."

"Marsha? This is Stacy. Can you meet me tonight? I have some news I think you'll be interested in."

I sat up straighter. "Of course. I'm picking up a jeep from Officer Wilson. I can come over—"

"Don't say anything to him about meeting me, okay? You can't trust…" Her phone crackled.

"Trust who? Hello?"

More static. "Know…map…watching." Her voice lowered. "I really think---Gotta go. Meet me at eight o'clock … football field." Click.

I stared at the receiver. "That was weird."

"Who called?" Mom asked.

"That was Stacy. She has some information for me, but the phone kept cutting out. I'm supposed to meet her tonight at the football field."

"Do you want me to come with you?"

I shook my head. "I'll head over there after looking at the jeep." Could I trust Stacy? I thought so. Meeting her could be a trap, but what did she have to gain? Why lure me to the football field? If she wanted to hurt me, she could catch me on my way home from work. None of it made sense. The last place I wanted to meet anyone after dark was the field. The lights would be off since there was no game.

Was that why she'd chosen the spot? She needed a dark and secretive place? Maybe she did intend to bash my head in. "I think I do want you to come with me. No, never mind." If it was a trap, I didn't want Mom in harm's way. "Isn't there football practice tonight?"

"Yes. It's over at eight. Once you make up your

mind, let me know." Mom disappeared into the supply room.

There should still be people milling around the field when I met Stacy. Good. My nerves settled, and I set to work on my ham and cheese Panini sandwich. There was absolutely nothing to worry about in regards to meeting Stacy. Especially since Mom knew where I would be going, and I'd let Duane know. I'd be perfectly safe.

*

I arrived at the field at a quarter to eight in my new-to-me red jeep iand, since I didn't see Stacy's car, sat in the bleachers to watch the last few minutes of practice. Duane glanced my way and waved. As a teenager, I'd spent many an evening doing the very same thing, except Duane was one of the boys practicing and not the coach.

At two minutes until eight, I clomped my way down the bleachers. Stacy had said football field in her call. Had she meant the bleachers, behind the restrooms, the snack bar? As the football players jogged off the field, I moved to the track that circled the field of green. There was no way Stacy could miss me now. I was the only person around.

A chilly breeze ruffled my hair, and I pulled my dark hoodie closer around me. Soon, the lights would go out, and I'd be truly alone on a massive field. The idea didn't appeal to me.

"Hey, beautiful."

I turned to greet Duane. "Hey yourself. You haven't seen Stacy, have you? I'm supposed to meet her here."

"Really?" His eyebrows rose. "I thought you

couldn't stand her."

"We have a truce. She really wants to help solve the murder of Mrs. Grimes." I shrugged. "Who am I to say no?"

He drew me close for a quick kiss. "Meet me in the parking lot when you're finished. We can grab a quick bite somewhere. I'm starving." He released me and loped in the direction of the boy's locker room.

I turned in a slow circle. Where was Stacy? It was now ten after eight. I decided to leave the field and check the more secret places. My footsteps were muffled as I left the rubber track, lending to the mood that I was the only person left in River Valley. Until I heard raised voices from under the visitor's side bleachers.

Changing direction, I increased my pace across the field. I'd reached the halfway point when the lights went out and the sprinklers came on. You have got to be kidding me! I dashed across the field and skid to a halt on the other side.

Water dripped from the ends of my hair onto my already soaked shirt. I needed to find Stacy fast before I froze to death. "Stacy!"

"Marsha, help!" Her cry came from the far end.

I grabbed one of the poles they used to mark where the football landed during the game and dashed to the rescue. Since I had nothing on me but my car keys and cell phone, any weapon was better than none.

Footsteps pounded. Mine or someone else's. I careened around the corner of the bleachers.

Stacy lay on her back, a knife protruding from

her chest. She reached out a hand for me. I dropped the flagged pole and fell to my knees before digging in my pocket for my phone. I sent Duane a quick text and then dialed 911.

"You're … next." Stacy gripped my shirt and pulled me down. "Said … watch …your back."

I glanced behind me as spiders skittered up my spine. "Who said that?"

"911 what is your emergency."

"I'm at the River Valley football field. Visitor side bleachers. Someone stabbed Stacy Tate in the heart."

"Where is that person now?"

"Stacy or the killer?" Because it was now a second murder. Stacy's lifeless gaze penetrated mine even as her chest failed to rise with another breath.

"Police and medical personnel are on their way. Please stay on the phone."

"Hurry." I whipped my head from one direction to the other fast enough to give me whip lash. Stacy's whispered warning would haunt my dreams. I was next. How long did I have?

A car door slammed from the direction of the parking lot. The killer was leaving, I hoped. Still, I scooted to a spot where bars that held up the bleachers crisscrossed in a thick enough pattern it would be hard for someone to sneak up and stab me in the back.

"Ma'am, are you there?"

"I'm here." My throat constricted. My breath came in gasps.

"Are you in danger?"

"I don't know! I'm sitting here next to a dead body. I very well could be in danger."

"Is there a safe place you can go?"

"Not without stepping out into the open." Who was this woman? Why did she keep asking me questions? Conversation was the last thing on my mind. Oh, God, please keep me alive.

Sirens pierced the night. Blue and red flashes of light filled the parking lot with false gaiety.

A hand landed on my shoulder.

I screamed and dropped my phone.

"Shh. It's me." Duane pulled me into his hands as the operator screamed if I were all right. "Are you okay?"

I buried my face in his shirt as Bruce and Officer Bradford charged under the bleachers. Behind them came three paramedics with a stretcher. "Stacy is dead. I got here seconds after she was stabbed."

His arms tightened around me. Nothing on earth made me feel safer than Duane. "I've got you. Let's get out from under here and wait for Bruce up top. Why are you soaked?"

I'd forgotten about my drenching, but now I shivered with a force hard enough to clank my teeth together. "I got caught on the field."

Duane set me on a bleacher than raced away, returning seconds later with a stadium blanket. He wrapped it around my shoulders, and then pulled me close. "I'm sorry I didn't get here sooner. I tried, but one of the boys needed his ankle taped, and—"

"It's okay. I should have texted something more than I need your help. We need a code word or something for when it's imperative you get to me."

He sighed. "Considering your talent for finding danger and dead bodies, I guess we do."

"Danger. That's all I'll say or text." I laid my cheek against his chest and breathed deep of a musky cologne and a manly scent that was all Duane I closed my eyes to the sight of Stacy's body being wheeled from under the bleachers.

Who would write about River Valley's simple lifestyle now? Who would alert the town that another murder had been committed? Tears burned their way down my frigid cheeks. Poor Stacy only lasted a day in the sleuthing business. I must keep my guardian angel working overtime.

"Bruce is coming." Duane whispered in my ear. "I'll stay right here while he badgers you."

"Thank you. He'll be less of a jerk if you're here." I opened my eyes and straightened.

Bruce resembled a bandy rooster all puffed chest and squinty eyes. It did bother me that I kept the poor man on his toes with the trouble I got into, but must he look at me as if it were all my fault?

14

"I knew as soon as the call came in that I'd find Marsha here." Bruce stared down at us, shaking his head. "Tell me you didn't touch the handle of the knife."

"I didn't touch it. I didn't even touch her." I shuddered. Seeing more than one dead body had taught me a few things about police procedure. I wasn't a total imbecile.

"Can this wait until morning?" Duane asked. "It's been a tough night for Marsha."

"No, it cannot." Bruce pulled a notepad from his pocket. "I know from prior experience that Marsha forgets to come to the station to fill out a report, and I have to chase her down. We'll do it now."

"It's okay." I patted Duane's arm. "I'd rather get it over with."

"What were you doing here?" Bruce poised his pen over the paper.

"I was supposed to meet Stacy. She called and said she had something to tell me about Mrs. Grimes's death." I cringed at the hard look that came over Bruce's face.

"Did she tell you?"

I shook my head. "She had already been stabbed by the time I found her."

"Any glimpse of her attacker?"

"No. I did hear a car door slam when I was beside her. Before she died, Stacy told me I was next."

"Next for what?"

"To be killed, most likely." Did I need to spell everything out for him? "Maybe the killer told her to tell me."

"Right before they stabbed her in the heart. Right." Bruce snapped his notepad closed. "Most killers don't warn their victims."

"I don't really think Stacy had a reason to lie."

Bruce glared at me for a moment before speaking. "I don't know what to think anymore. Duane, keep her out of my way or I will arrest her for the sake of herself and this town." He spun on his heel and marched away.

That wasn't the first time he'd threatened to arrest me. By now, it was just part of the game we played. Keeping the blanket around my shoulders, I stood. "I'd rather go home than out somewhere to eat. I need to get into some dry clothes. Do you want to follow me?"

"I'd follow you anywhere." Duane tweaked my nose. "Don't worry about Bruce. He's frustrated because he can't find the person responsible for these deaths. It does bother me that you've been given a warning from the killer, though."

That made both of us. Of course, again, not the first time I'd gotten a warning from someone out to prevent me from finding out their identity.

Duane escorted me to my car, made sure I'd locked the doors, and handed me my cell phone through the window. "Thought you might want this. Roll up the window. Love you."

"Thanks, I love you, too." I'd forgotten about my dropped phone. "See you at the house."

After setting the jeep's heater to high, I pulled out of the parking lot and headed for home, keeping my eyes peeled through my rearview mirror for a dark sedan. I was so focused on someone that might be following me that I cruised through a stop sign. A horn blared, startling me into paying attention.

I gasped and tightened my grip on the wheel to prevent from swerving onto the sidewalk. Lindsey screamed and threw her backpack at me. I stomped on the brake and rushed from the car.

"I'm so sorry. I wasn't looking where I was going." I could have killed my daughter!

"That's obvious." Lindsey retrieved her pack from the jeep's hood and opened the passenger side door. "Since you're here, you can give me a ride home. It's the least you can do after almost running me over."

True. I slid back behind the steering wheel. "I found Stacy Tate dead tonight. Well, she wasn't dead until after I found her, but she's ... dead."

"Did you kill her?"

"Of course not." Gee. What did my daughter think of me? I steered the car back onto the road. "I got there moments before she died. The killer had already disappeared."

"Well, you didn't really like her."

I glanced sharply in her direction. "Do you kill everyone you don't like?"

"No, but I don't get in near the trouble you do." She huffed and bounced back against the seat. "And I'm the teenager. Sometimes, I feel like the adult."

Ouch. It did seem as if I sniffed out trouble. I guess this time, I did. The first time, I was defending Lindsey against unjust accusations. The second time, a victim had come to me for help. This time…I'd willingly offered to stick my nose where it didn't belong all because of a book fair.

I pulled into our driveway. It wasn't as if Mrs. Grimes asked me to continue after her death. It had been Mr. Dean who had made the request—my top suspect. Could he have wanted me in harm's way in order to keep attention off himself for some reason I hadn't yet thought of?

Lindsey slammed her car door shut and marched into the house. No lights glowed from the windows, letting me know that Mom was back in the guesthouse settling in for the night. I really wanted to brainstorm my next move with someone other than my sixteen-year-old daughter.

I smiled, remembering the one person always there for me to talk to. I turned off the car lights, locked the doors, and closed my eyes. "God, take this burden from me. It's not my place to hunt down a killer." Of course, there was the fact that the killer made contact shortly after I decided to take over the book fair, but I could have stopped investigating. "I've gone and put myself in a dangerous situation again. Please, protect me from myself and this crazy person out to get me."

Someone banged on the window. I screeched and tried to duck to the floorboard. I might have made it, too, if I hadn't had my seatbelt holding me back.

"What in the world are you doing?" Mom pressed her face against the glass. "I thought you were dead. It almost gave me a heart attack."

I opened the door and slid out. "I was praying."

"Well, the good book says you are to pray without ceasing and all, but when there is a killer running around threatening you, I'd hope you'd have better sense than to sit in the dark with your eyes closed. What's wrong with praying in the house?" She matched her pace with mine as I went inside.

"No one was around and I needed some alone time." I dropped my keys in the ceramic dish I kept on the foyer table.

"You're distraught because you found Stacy dead." Mom patted my arm. "I understand."

"How do you know about that already?" News traveled fast in this town. I headed straight to the kitchen and climbed on the counter to get to my M&Ms. Silly, really. I might as well keep them down where I could reach them. Putting them up high didn't dissuade me in the least.

"Duane got held up at the field and called to ask me to check up on you." Mom headed to the coffee pot and filled it with water. "I wasn't in bed yet. A body needs less sleep the older you get."

I told Mom about Stacy's last words. Her eyes widened, and she closed the kitchen curtains. "Too bad she couldn't squeeze in the killer's name in there."

"My thoughts exactly. It had to be someone Stacy knew. I heard loud voices, then a scream. If it had been a stranger, wouldn't she have cried out earlier?" I popped several candies in my mouth. "How hard is it to stab someone?"

"How would I know?" Mom set the pot in the coffee maker. "I'm pretty sure I could do it, though. Here." She pulled a thick roast from the refrigerator. "Stab away."

"It doesn't have skin on it. That's the toughest part of a human body other than the bones." I shuddered.

"True, but it will give you an idea." She held out a butcher knife.

I wrapped my hand around the handle, raised it above my head, and stabbed. There was a little more resistance than I'd thought. If you add a layer of skin and clothing, it still wasn't too difficult for the average person. I gave another stab for good measure.

"Oh. My. Gosh." Lindsey stopped in the doorway. "What are you doing now?"

"Your mother wants to know what it feels like to stab someone," Mom offered.

"Are you taking into account that you're most likely looking into that person's eyes and that they're begging you to stop?" My daughter watched too much Criminal Minds. "That would cause an average person to hesitate."

So, we were looking for someone with so much to lose that pleading made little difference to them. I set the knife in the sink and wrapped the roast in aluminum foil. We could still use it for sandwiches.

"I paid a visit to the tea room again." Mom poured herself a cup of coffee and offered me one. I shook my head. "Norma Rae is in sad financial trouble. Although we see her and Ingrid together a lot, the two do not get along. Norma Rae pretty much uses the guilt trip to get her daughter to do things with her. If her business fails, she will have to move in with Ingrid. A fate worse than death, she said."

A motive for murder, maybe. Mr. Dean wanted his affair with Mrs. Grimes kept secret. I pulled my note taking pad from the drawer and scanned the list. The Snyder's had a gambling problem, or so the rumor went, and Mrs. Willis wanted to retire and write murder mysteries. I crossed her name off the suspect list. Her only motive for killing would be for research purposes. No one did that, did they? How could I get a look at her manuscript?

Another few pieces of candy went in my mouth. "Does Norma Rae strike you as a strong person? It would take a bit of strength to choke someone."

"Have you seen the trays she carries?" Mom blew into her mug.

"Mrs. Willis looks like she could strangle someone."

"She's fat," Lindsey said. "Really big. She probably can't move fast, but I bet she's as strong as an ox."

Instead of illuminating suspects, we were only making their motivations and means stronger. "This is going nowhere."

"Eventually we'll stumble across something that

will make sense," Mom said. "You should know that by now.

"I usually figure out the killer right about the time they kidnap me."

Mom nodded. "We really need to stop that from happening. You know what they say about third times."

"That it's a charm?"

"Hello, ladies." Duane waltzed into the room, kissing me, then planting a kiss on Mom's and Lindsey's cheeks. "Why so serious?"

"We're discussing how it's about time for Marsha's luck to run out." Mom set her cup in the sink. "She's bound and determined to make me old before my time. As much as I enjoy helping her solve these mysteries, she's the only one unlucky enough to be targeted by the killer."

"Which is fine by me." Tears stung my eyes. "I couldn't live if something happened to any of you."

"Nothing is going to happen to any of us," Duane said. He glared at each one of us. "Risk or not, Marsha goes nowhere alone. Ever."

"It won't matter," Mom challenged his stare. "She wasn't alone when run off the road. We might as well lock her in her room."

Then the killer would probably burn the house down around me. I was counting on the treasure hunt on Saturday to clear up some things. If not, Mom could very well be right. I had a bomb on my back and the counter was ticking down.

15

I studied the piles of water bottles and granola bars. Did I really want to close the store on a Saturday and go on a wild goose chase across the state of Arkansas for a treasure that had been searched for by everyone and their grandfather? Not really. It seemed more beneficial for the purpose of finding the killer by spreading the little white lie that we may have found a treasure.

"That backpack isn't going to pack itself," Mom said, coming into the kitchen with her arms loaded with hats. "It's going to be a warm day so I dug these out of storage."

"I don't think we should waste our time." I explained to her my reasons.

"Good. We're getting behind at work." Mom dumped the hats on the table. "When one of our loose-lipped neighbors come into the store, we'll let the news slip about a map. That's sure to draw the mice out of the cupboards."

My sentiments exactly. I texted Duane to let him know Mom and I were working instead. Since Lindsey hadn't crawled out of bed yet, I didn't expect any arguments out of her. Duane texted back almost immediately saying the timing was perfect … it was his Saturday to watch detention students and he was having a hard time finding someone to take his place.

Men. It might've been a better idea to have started looking for a replacement earlier in the week. I changed direction and made a sandwich to take to work while I prayed my bad mood would disappear.

Mom was right. We had loads of work to do with the holiday season almost upon us, and I had a few more things to line up for the book fair slash harvest festival. Right after I made a couple of stuffed Christmas trees and quilted ornaments.

Feeling my stress levels rising by the minute, I grabbed my purse. "See you at the store. Would you leave Lindsey a note, please?" I dashed outside and into my jeep.

Ten minutes later, I was unlocking the back door to the shop. I stored my purse in a cabinet in the back of the shop and headed to the front. I stopped and surveyed the mess.

The store was ransacked. The shattered front door mocked me. I sagged against the counter. Who would do this? If someone had it out for me, why hurt my livelihood? I put a hand over my mouth. What if they were still here?

I grabbed the broom behind the counter. There weren't a lot of places to hide, but I wasn't taking any chances. A hand grabbed my arm. I whirled and swung, slamming the broom against my daughter's shoulder.

She yelled and sagged to her knees. "Why did you hit me?"

"What are you doing here?" I dropped next to her, my gaze sweeping the room. "Where were you?"

"In the bathroom. When I heard someone trashing the store, I hid. I tried to call the police but my phone is dead." She clutched her shoulder while tears coursed down her cheek.

"I'm so sorry." What if I would have hit her in the head? What if I broke her collar bone? I was a horrible mother. Who hits their child with a broom handle?

"I've been coming in early on the weekends to work on a present for your wedding day." Lindsey scooted against the counter. "While I was in the bathroom, I heard someone come through the back door. No one but family has a key to that door. I thought I'd be safe." She glared at me through her tears. "Boy, was I wrong."

"I'm so sorry." I dropped the broom and wiped away her tears with my thumbs. "Let me call Bruce and I'll get you to the hospital. Why today? We had plans."

"I figured I'd be back before you got out of bed." She rocked back and forth. "It doesn't pay to be nice to you."

I stood and grabbed the phone off the counter and dialed Bruce's personal number. "There's been a break in at Country Gifts, and I've injured my daughter. We need you."

He sighed. "I'll be there in five minutes."

After I hung up the phone I sat next to Lindsey

and wrapped my arms around her. She yelped and scooted away. "Don't touch me."

While we waited, I paced the floor, taking in the destruction. Hand blown glass ornaments crunched under my feet. Quilts lay in piles on the floor. The consignment corner shelves were empty, its contents strewn. It could have been a warning…instinct told me someone was looking for something. How stupid to think I'd hide something of importance among the merchandise.

Bruce pulled into the parking spot in front of the store, lights blazing. At least he hadn't run the siren. He exited the squad car and approached the store with one hand on the gun at his skinny hip. He used a rag to open the front door. Locked. He glared at me.

I shrugged and rushed to let him in. I was used to his looks. "Sorry."

"Anything missing?" he asked.

"I have no idea." I gestured around the shop. "It's a total disaster. Mom and I will be out of business for a few days," if there's even anything of value left to sell."

Speaking of Mom, she rushed through the back door. "What in heaven's name…Oh, sweetie." She plopped next to Lindsey. "Were you attacked?"

"Yes. By Mom."

Mom whirled. "Why would you strike your daughter?"

"It was an accident. I thought she was the intruder."

"You're a menace." Bruce brushed past me. "Do you want me to call an ambulance?"

"No." My shoulders sagged. "I'll take her to the hospital myself as soon as you're finished here."

Bruce pulled out his infernal notepad. "Why did you suspect your daughter to be the culprit?"

"She came up behind me." I crossed my arms. "I'd just seen the store and grabbed a broom in case the guilty person was still here. It was a reflex action. She said she was hiding in the bathroom while the store was being trashed."

He nodded. "You didn't see the person responsible?" he directed at her.

"No. They didn't say anything. I heard the glass break and almost came out, but then I could tell they were throwing things around." She sniffed and, using the wall for support, slid to her feet. "I think there was more than one person, but I'm not sure."

"What makes you think that?"

"The footsteps sounded different. These walls are pretty thin. It's actually kind of embarrassing if you need to use the restroom when customers are here."

Bruce raised his eyebrows. "Let's stay on topic, shall we?"

"Make it quick, Bruce. My daughter is in pain." Yes, it was my fault, but there was no sense in making her suffer longer than necessary. We should have gone on the treasure hunt.

Officer Bradford joined us and set to work taking notes on the condition of the store. Personal experience had taught me that the store would be closed for a few days while they did their investigation. No need for us to be fingerprinted. We were experienced at how the legal system worked. Our prints were already on file.

"What have you been getting into, Marsha? Anything you haven't told me?" Bruce speared me a glance.

"No, we haven't even started to spread any—" Oh, no.

"Any what?" His face reddened.

"Nothing."

"I can tell from the tone in your voice it's anything but nothing. Don't make me call Duane."

Oh, the man played dirty. "We were going to spread a little rumor around town that we'd found a treasure. You know, to flush out the bad guy."

"You enjoy starting fires, don't you?" He shook his head. "Don't forget what I said about meddling in my investigation."

How could I? He brought it up every time we were in close proximity with each other. "I haven't. Spreading rumors isn't against the law."

"Why do you insist on putting yourself in danger? Do you have a death wish?"

"Of course not. Can we go now?"

"Not yet. Have a seat over there while we look around."

"There's no one else here."

"We'll be the judge of that."

I rolled my eyes and sat in a rocking chair next to one Lindsey claimed. Mom's eyes flitted from one corner of the room to the other. No doubt she itched to start cleaning and taking inventory. I felt the same way.

Tears escaped and I rubbed my face on the sleeve of my blouse. Crying wouldn't solve anything. Only time spent in prayer and a brainstorming session with the family would divulge any results. Mom's hands might be aching to hold a broom, but my fingers hungered over wanting a pen and sheets of paper. Two people, possibly.

I stared out the window toward the street. Kids, maybe? It was quite possible the break-in had nothing to do with Mrs. Grimes's death. If it did, what suspects did we have that were pairs? Norma Rae and Ingrid, Janet and Brad Snyder, those were the only ones. All of whom could have walked up to Stacy on the football field and not raised an alarm in her mind.

Of course, the killer could have hired a couple of teens to wreck the place. River Valley didn't have many wayward youth, but there were a few who fancied themselves big city gangers. How could I find out? Lynn had already promised to try and get information from the high school teachers. I doubted she'd want to question the students.

They probably wouldn't talk to her anyway. If students behaved as they did when I was in school, not many young people saw teachers as a confidant. Especially when breaking the law. Maybe Duane could put feelers out with the football team.

I straightened at the sight of Sarah Boatwright staring through the shattered door. Our gazes met for a second before she marched down the sidewalk. Curious. Why hadn't she asked how we were?

Lindsey moaned. "I'm thirsty."

I leaped to my feet and rushed to fetch her water from the refrigerator in the back. Enough was enough. I grabbed a bottle of water and my purse, then rushed to where Bruce studied a footprint outside the back door.

"This yours?" he asked.

"No." The shoe print was larger and the sole was smooth. The shoes I currently wore had a geometric pattern on the bottom. "I'm taking Lindsey to the doctor. She's in pain and I'm not having her wait any longer. You know where we are if you need us."

"Right. Put your foot next to the print but don't touch the dirt." He pointed.

I hovered my foot over the print. I'd been mistaken. They were the same size. So were Mom's and Lindsey's. Mom was wearing ballet flats and Lindsey Converses. "It could be Mom's print. Mom?"

She came outside and Bruce had her do the same thing he'd asked me to do. Then he had her step in a soft patch of dirt a few feet away. The prints didn't match. Finally, a clue. I met Bruce's gaze over Mom's head. We were looking for a woman.

"Don't go and do anything stupid, Marsha." Bruce jangled the handcuffs on his belt. "You may now take your daughter to the doctor."

"Well, thank you very much."

Mom bent over the print that didn't belong to any of us. I joined her, not really knowing what I was looking for but something about the print seemed off.

The toe of the right foot was deeper. "Are we looking for someone who is pigeon-toed?"

Mom shrugged. "I'm not an investigator, but you can bet I'll be studying people's shoes more than usual."

So would I. We were getting close. It was a race between us and a killer. Who will find who first?

16

"I'm hungry," Lindsey said. "Can we stop for a burger?"

"I thought you were in pain." I turned into the Emergency Room lot.

"Not anymore. It barely hurts now."

She must be in shock. Bruce had kept us waiting too long. I turned off the engine and exited the jeep. Mom was opening Lindsey's door before I moved around the vehicle.

"We're going to have you checked out anyway," Mom said, glaring at me. "Your mother has a good swing when she wants to. You could have a fracture."

"I said it was an accident." I followed them through the emergency room doors. "You would have done the same."

"I. Would. Never. Hit. My child." With her nose in the air, Mom marched up to the counter.

To prevent her from opening her mouth and having me arrested for child abuse, I shouldered her aside. "My daughter needs her shoulder x-rayed."

"Name." The woman never looked up.

Seriously, the customer service at some places.

"Lindsey Steele."

"Have a seat in the waiting room."

Ten people waited on green plastic chairs. We'd be here all day. Maybe urgent care would have been a better idea. We took our seats, Lindsey eyeing the vending machine. I dug in my purse for some change and handed it over.

"I'll get it for you, sweetie." Mom took the money. "You sit there and rest."

For heaven's sake. I punched Duane's number into my phone and got his voice mail. I left him a message telling him where we were then reclined against the back of the chair.

Waiting rooms were full of germs. We'd probably all have the flu by the time we left. "Don't touch anything," I whispered to Lindsey.

"They have hand sanitizer over there." She pointed to the front desk. "Relax."

I fidgeted, eyeing the other patients. One man looked as if he could die at any minute. His eyes were closed. A bloody bandage wrapped around his hand. Why was he still sitting here? The one time I'd been rushed to the hospital for eating a poisonous cookie, they'd taken me straight back. At least I thought so. I had been a little out of touch with reality.

Closing my eyes, I leaned my head back and listened to Mom baby talk my sixteen-year-old. The surprising thing was that Lindsey allowed her to. I guess the benefit of a grandmother willing to wait on you hand and foot because your mother tried to kill you was a good thing.

Lips plastered against mine. I swung, my fist

connecting with Duane's cheek. "Oh, my gosh! I'm so sorry."

"Don't worry, Uncle Duane. She's a bit jumpy lately. Almost killed me at the store." Lindsey reached up for a hug from him.

"What?" He sent me a questioning glance over my daughter's head.

I sighed. "The store was broken into and trashed. I had a broom in my hand as a defense in case the perps were still in the store. When Lindsey came up behind me, I reacted without thinking and hit her." Much like I'd done when Duane snuck up and kissed me.

He released Lindsey and grabbed my arm to pull me a few feet to the side. Lowering his voice, he said, "Are you all right? You're strung tighter than a guitar string. This mystery is too much for you."

"No, I'm fine. It was a shock seeing the store like that, and well, with all that's happened this year, I tend to react before thinking." The concern in his eyes was almost my undoing. I'd back out of finding the murderer if I could, but I was in too deep.

"Lindsey Steele." A nurse appeared in a side door.

After planting a quick kiss on Duane's lips, I followed the nurse and Lindsey through the door. Mom scuttled after us.

"I'll wait out here," Duane called.

The nurse led us to a curtained alcove and proceeded to take Lindsey's blood pressure. "What are we seeing you for today?"

"She needs her shoulder x-rayed," Mom said.

"She was hit with a broomstick."

"A broomstick?" The nurse glanced at me.

"It was an accident. She startled me." I plopped in the padded vinyl chair beside the bed. "Someone had just broken into our business."

The nurse narrowed her eyes and studied my daughter. "Does your mother make a habit of hitting you? Don't be afraid to answer truthfully. You're in a safe place."

Good grief. I rested my elbow on the chair's arm and plopped my chin in my hand. Now, I'd be labeled an abusive mother. Add that to my resume.

Lindsey giggled. "No, she usually just yells."

"She verbally abuses you?"

Lindsey's smile faded. "No, that's not what I meant. Really, my life is good. Very good."

The nurse expelled a sharp breath out her nose. "If you decide that isn't the story you want to stick with, you can call the local police or this clinic for help." She undid the blood pressure cuff. "I'll get the doctor."

Tears welled in Lindsey's eyes. "I'm sorry, Mom. I didn't mean to—"

"I know, sweetie. The nurse is only doing her job." I straightened and waited for the doctor to arrive with his own myriad of questions.

Thirty minutes later, clipboard in hand, he shoved aside the curtain. "Lindsey? Let's take a look at you shall we? Would you like your mother and grandmother to give us a bit of privacy?"

"We aren't going anywhere, doctor." Mom crossed her arms. "You'll only ask her more stupid questions about being an abused child. Which. She.

Is. Not."

This wasn't helping. "Do you want us to leave?" I put a hand on my daughter's arm.

"No." Lindsey paled.

The doctor felt around the area of her shoulder I'd hit, then rotated the arm. "Everything seems fine. It's most likely bruised but an x-ray won't hurt."

"You can x-ray me if my mom comes, too." Lindsey lifted her chin.

That's my girl. Loyal to the end.

The doctor sighed. "I don't think an x-ray is necessary. I see here you don't have insurance." He peered closer at me. "Weren't you in here a few months ago?" His eyes widened. "I recognize you now. You're the local sleuth." He shook his head. "It all makes sense now. I'll get the release papers together." He shoved aside the curtain again and left.

"His bedside manner is sadly lacking." Mom peered around the curtain. "I'm thinking that if you're going to continue chasing killers, you might want to think about medical insurance."

Probably not a bad idea. "Who do you think broke into the store? Do you think it was a warning?"

"I don't know." Mom leaned against the wall. "They didn't take anything. Not even cash from the register."

"Somebody knows we have the map." I got up and paced the small cubicle. "They may even think we have the treasure. Have you told anyone?"

"Not yet. There hasn't been time. Besides,

Bruce has the original."

"I don't think it matters. Even the copy shows where the supposed treasure is."

"Hot Springs isn't exactly a small town," Mom said. "That treasure could be anywhere around there."

There was a definitive X marking the spot. A hunter would check there first.

Quick footsteps passed on the other side of the curtain. A voice yelled out for someone to look where they were going.

Mom peeked around the curtain again. "Where is that doctor? Oh, here he is."

"You ladies are free to go. The shoulder will be bruised for a few days, but ibuprofen should help alleviate the pain. No more swinging brooms, Mrs. Steele."

"I'll do my best." I helped Lindsey off the bed, relieved I hadn't done her serious damage.

Duane was reading a Good Housekeeping magazine when we joined him in the waiting room. Next to him, Leroy read over his shoulder. Upon sight of us, Duane dropped the magazine on a nearby table and stood. "I can't believe women actually read that kind of stuff. There wasn't a single sports story in there."

I chuckled. "That's because women are more interested in recipes, keeping a nice home, and looking pretty."

"Everything okay?" He glanced at Lindsey.

"Yes. She's bruised, but that will heal." I slipped my arm through his. "She's also craving a burger."

"Wanda's Diner?"

"Sounds good. We haven't been there in a long time." Lindsey dashed out the door. My daughter would be just fine, and my guilt over her injury would also fade.

Several minutes later, we all met at the diner and slid into a large corner booth. Through the window, I could see the giant plaster cow that served as a town landmark. That atrocity loomed over the parking lot for the past thirty years. Having once been a barbecue place, Wanda hadn't wanted to tear it down when she bought the place. Said it added character.

Wanda strolled up to our table. "Good afternoon. I'm a bit short-handed today. My part-time waitress burned herself in the kitchen and had to go to the ER. What can I get you folks?"

"Bacon cheeseburgers all around," Leroy said.

"I'm looking for a part-time job," Lindsey said.

"Perfect. You take the job, and today's burgers are on the house." Wanda beamed. "Noon to six on Saturdays and Sundays sound good to you? There might be other times I'll need your help, but we can start with those days."

"I can start tomorrow." Lindsey practically bounced in her seat.

"Wonderful. You're hired." Wanda put her order pad in the pocket of her apron and rushed off to fetch our orders.

Lindsey usually helped Mom and I at Country Gifts but I wouldn't take away her joy at having a real job for anything. She'd still be available for an hour or two each day after school if we needed her.

"Good job, kid." Duane clapped her on her shoulder. She winced. He grimaced and apologized.

"I wonder who got burned?" Mom glanced toward the kitchen. "I haven't heard of any new help here at the diner."

"That Jennings girl," Leroy said. "The one who also works at the station. I heard she works here on the weekends."

"Whatever for?"

He shrugged. "I guess she needs the money."

Wanda arrived with iced teas all around. "Food will be ready in about ten minutes."

"Is your help Ingrid Jennings?" Mom asked.

"Yep. I don't like to talk bad about people," Wanda said. "but she's a sullen gal. I'll probably fire her now that Lindsey's here. I'll give her a few more days to change her attitude. If that doesn't happen, I'm giving her the boot. I don't care if she'll have to live with her mother or not."

The wheels in my head were spinning faster than a Tilt-A-Whirl. I sipped my sweet tea and stared out the window.

On the sidewalk outside, Mr. Dean and Mrs. Willis appeared to be in a heated discussion. He stood with his hands deep in his pockets, while her arms flailed with each word. I'd never seen the English teacher so animated. The scene was better than any television drama and served to pull me away from the financial problems of the Jennings. By the time our food arrived, they'd stalked off in opposite directions.

Full from lunch and ready for a relaxing afternoon, I drove home, minus my daughter who decided to stay and observe Wanda. Mom would be home after running errands with Leroy and Duane headed back to the high school.

I pulled the jeep into the driveway and was greeted by Cleopatra. I patted her head. "Who let you out of the backyard?" If Lindsey left the gate open, we'd have some words when she got home. "Come on, girl."

She followed me up the porch and into a house as trashed as the store.

17

After a sleepless weekend and time spent listening to Bruce warn me about an arrest again, the ringing of my cell phone on my nightstand was not a welcome sound. I groped for it, knocking it to the floor, thus having to get mostly out of bed to retrieve it. "Hello? This better be good."

"I'm pretty sure you'll think it is," Lynn said. "How soon can you be at the school? My prep time is in fifteen minutes."

"What is it?" I scooted to a sitting position against the headboard.

"I've got a copy of Mrs. Willis's manuscript. Believe me, you want to see this."

"I'm leaving now." I hung up, yanked on a pair of jeans under the large tee-shirt I wore to bed, and then slipped my feet into flats. Grabbing my purse, I was out of the house in less than five minutes.

I made it to the school five minutes before Lynn's prep time. The bell rang and thirty high school students barged from her class, allowing me to slip into her room. "How did you get it?"

"Hello to you, too." Lynn moved to a filing cabinet and pulled out a thick stack of paper. "My school laptop crashed and I had to get a new one. Seems like Estelle had the same problem a week or so ago. When they fixed hers, they forgot to wipe the drive clean. I ended up with her old one, and voila! A copy of her murder mystery. I've highlighted the spots I think you might be interested in." She handed the stack to me.

I sat at one of the desks and riffled through the pages. The first highlighted spot was about the victim, an elderly woman, being killed with a silk scarf. I glanced up at Lynn. She motioned for me to continue. Farther on in the story, another victim died of a stab wound in the heart. My heart thudded like the high school marching band drummer.

"This is huge."

Lynn grinned. "I thought so."

"I saw Mr. Dean and Mrs. Willis arguing yesterday outside of Wanda's Diner. Do you know what about?" I stacked the manuscript back into a neat pile. I'd take it to Bruce at the first opportunity.

"Probably because she wants out of her contract." Lynn sat back at her desk. "She's convinced her novel will be a bestseller and says she can't write and promote while working a day job. She'll really leave the senior students in a bind if she quits."

I could see where that would upset him, but there really wasn't anything he could do if she was willing to pay the fee for opting out of her contract. "Can I take this with me? I think Bruce should have it."

"Sure." Lynn laughed. "I have a copy on my laptop. It's not a bad read, really."

Maybe not, but the closeness of her story to what was happening in River Valley was too much of a coincidence to me. It seemed as if the woman might be killing people in the name of research.

I shoved the stack of papers in my purse and headed to the library. Since I was at the school, I might as well check on the progress of the book fair. It was only a little over a week away. There were more fliers to count and pass out, suggested decorations to pour over, and Mrs. Grimes's antique books still sat on the desk. What in the world was I to do with them?

I found an empty box in the back storeroom and stacked the books inside. Hefting the heavy load, I staggered to Mr. Dean's office and plopped the load on his desk. "These are some of Mrs. Grimes's personal belongings. I have no idea what to do with them."

"And you think I do?" He leaned back in his chair.

"I know the two of you had a relationship at one time. You're the closest thing to family I can find. Do with them what you will." I turned to go.

"How did you find out?" His eyes clouded with pain.

I glanced over my shoulder. "Secrets aren't really secrets in a school, Mr. Dean." I left his office and approached Cheryl's desk. I was still curious about why she'd come to the store on Saturday morning, only to leave without saying a word.

"Was there something you needed?" I tilted my head. "Surely you noticed the destruction of my store, yet you pranced on by as if everything were normal."

She paled. "There wasn't anything I could do other than get in the way." She handed me a sheet of paper. "Here is a list of everything for the fair. All that is needed is the tunnel to be built. Norma Rae has said she will even dress up as a knife wielding maniac. The other members of the book club will run the actual book sales. Will there be anything else?"

I shook my head. "I'll get Leroy started on building the tunnel this weekend. Could you put the word out that we'll need a last minute meeting on Friday? Six o'clock in the library?"

"Will do." She turned and grabbed her phone.

Effectively dismissed, I headed back to the library as a swarm of students entered the doors. A young woman who looked fresh out of college sat behind the desk. She introduced herself as the long-term substitute. I grabbed my purse and told her to call me if she needed the book fair crates moved or she could feel free to have some of the students shove them in a corner.

Still in a tiff that I had no excuse for, I rushed back to the parking lot. My poor attitude shamed me. Sure I was suffering from lack of sleep, but it gave me no reason to purposely antagonize people. The very people who might already want to kill me.

Behind the wheel of my jeep, I closed my eyes and prayed for peace. God was the only one who could settle my nerves and steady my mind. Duane was right. This case was too much for me. I'd give anything to be able to back out of my impulsive decision to continue with the book fair and solve the murder.

The prayer helped a little, but my eyelids felt heavy and sandy. Stressed out or not, I needed my cup of coffee before heading to the store. I drove to the coffee shop. I exited the jeep as Norma Rae was unlocking the front door to her tea shop down the street. I switched direction.

"Norma Rae!" I jogged to her side.

She frowned. "Yeah?"

"I heard Ingrid was injured yesterday. How is she?"

"Back at work at the station. She's fine." Norma Rae pushed open the door. "Needs to pay more attention to her surroundings is all. Did you need something? We aren't open yet."

The chill coming off her would freeze a southern lake. "No, just checking on Ingrid. Thanks for offering to help with the haunted tunnel."

"It'll be a blast." She grinned, the smile lacking warmth. I shuddered. Goose pimples broke out on my arms, and I hurried back to the coffee shop feeling as if I'd narrowly escaped the teeth of a shark.

Once I'd purchased my frozen mocha drink, I drove to the police station. Ingrid sat behind the counter, a white bandage around her left hand. "That looks painful."

"Not too bad. Are you here to see Bruce?"

"Yes, please." I wanted to get into a conversation with her, but how do you dig up someone's financial woes without hurting their feelings? I sipped my drink and avoided eye contact, which wasn't hard since she pretty much ignored me after telling Bruce I was there. After a few minutes, she told me to go on back.

"You can get into your shop today," Bruce said.

"Great! But that isn't why I'm here." I pulled the manuscript from my purse. "I managed to get my hands on a book written by Mrs. Estelle Willis. I think you'll be as interested in the highlighted areas as I am."

"I don't read."

Doesn't or can't? I smirked. "You'll want to read this."

He groaned and flipped through the pages. "Where did you get this?"

"I can't divulge my sources, but it's pretty interesting wouldn't you say?" I wiggled my eyebrows. "You can now add another suspect to your list."

"She's already a suspect because she worked with the victim." As if realizing he'd said too much, Bruce dropped the manuscript into a drawer. "Anything else?"

"I'd like to request a police presence at the harvest festival."

"Afraid someone will try to kill you?"

Yes. "There will be a lot of people there. Having the police in view will help prevent some of the shenanigans."

"We'd already planned on being there. Now, if you don't mind, I'm busy trying to find a killer."

"Any ideas on who trashed my home and work place?"

"Not yet, but the way you anger people, it could

be anyone."

Very funny. I left his office and called Mom on the way to my jeep to let her know we were allowed back into the shop. She said she'd meet me there in fifteen minutes to start cleaning.

I pulled into the alley behind the shop and stared at the back door. After the last fiasco, I was a bit apprehensive. I pulled my Taser out of my purse and kept it clutched tightly in my hand as I entered the store. Everything looked to be in the same sad state as on Saturday. Now that I wasn't feeling as if I'd permanently injured my daughter, tears filled my eyes at the destruction.

I shook out a quilt. Slivers of glass rained to the floor. None of the quilts or afghans could be sold until they were washed. The last thing we wanted was for someone to be cut. I stacked all the fabric goods on the counter, then started gathering anything else that was still in good condition. Everything glass was shattered on the floor in a rainbow of colors.

Grabbing the broom, I swept the shards into a pile as Mom marched into the room. "I've got most of it, if you want to start washing those things."

"Why are you crying?"

"I feel violated. Someone only suspects we have something they want and they're willing to ruin our belongings in order to find it. First here, then the house. Is nowhere sacred?" Why wouldn't the personal responsible confront me and get it over with?

"They let Cleopatra out of the back yard and locked up the cats in the bathroom. I could have lost my dog." I sniffed.

"At least they haven't started shooting at you." Mom took the broom from me. "Go sit down for a minute. I'll finish up."

"No, I need to stay busy."

"Marsha, you're on your last nerve. Sit down and drink your fancy coffee for fifteen minutes. Get a hold of yourself. There's plenty of work to be done."

I nodded. She was right. Once everything was cleaned up, maybe I wouldn't feel so assaulted. I sat in a rocking chair. "We need a security system."

"Leroy already has an appointment to have one installed here and at the house."

What a special man my mother had married. Almost as wonderful as the one I'd soon be wed to. I sipped my drink and rocked, turning again to prayer to calm me. A few minutes later, peace washed over me and I moved to help Mom restock the shelves with what we could. I flipped the sign on the window to open and propped the plywood covered door wide.

We could do this. Reopen, continue living, and catch a killer with no respect for life or property. The continue living was my favorite part.

18

Coffee in hand, I glanced at the calendar and groaned. The night of the book fair was approaching way too fast. Through the kitchen window, I could see several two by four studded boxes which Leroy would attach as rooms and hideaways on the huge tunnel he'd found somewhere. The tunnel actually looked like a large ventilation tube. He said with flickering lights and eerie sounds, along with rooms and scary characters, we'd have high school students scared to tears.

I shook my head. I wanted the kids to have fun, not scared out of their wits. But, if Lindsey's excitement was anything to go by each time she spotted Leroy's progress, the attraction would be a hit. I knew one thing…I had no intention of entering the tunnel.

"Good morning." Mom entered through the back door and headed right for the coffee pot.

"You love this kitchen, don't you?" Although the guest cottage, Mom and Leroy's home now after they gave the big house to me, had a small kitchenette, Mom still made regular trips to the house to cook and brew her coffee. "You can move back in. This house is too big for just Lindsey and me."

"No, no." Mom waved away the words. "After you're married to Duane, you may want to expand your family."

At the age of thirty-five, I doubted it. "I still think it's silly when you love this place like you do."

"I'm close enough." She pulled out a chair and joined me at the table. "You looked deep in thought when I came in."

"I'm trying to put the pieces of this puzzle together. None of our suspects have done anything to take suspicion off them. Also, did you notice how lopsided the kitchen drawer where I keep my notes is? I think the killer has seen the list." Which means they could suspect we're closer than we actually are. My family was in danger. I was in danger. "Maybe you and Leroy should take Lindsey on a small trip."

After the last mystery, they'd purchased a motor home for the times they wanted to travel the country. I'd feel better if they were far away from here for the next week or so.

"And miss all the fun? No thanks." Mom's smile didn't disguise the worry in her eyes. But, she was a trooper and only God reaching down and holding her still would keep her from helping her only child.

"Where do we go from here?" I got up and retrieved my clipboard from the broken drawer.

Mom wiggled her fingers to see the sheets of paper on the board. "Well, rumor has it that Janet and Brad Snyder paid off their gambling debts with help from his parents and are attending Gambler's Anonymous, so I think we can take them off the list." Mom penciled a line through their names. "There's also word that Officer Wilson is dating Ingrid Jennings. That doesn't necessarily make him a suspect, it only shows he has no sense."

I laughed. "Where do you get your information?"

"The craft club, where else? Actually, this time, Betty Larson called me. She and the ladies have been snooping."

God bless those silver-haired women. "What else?"

"Sarah Boatwright, the high school office manager quit after a dispute of some kind with Cheryl. Now, Cheryl is the office manager. Should we be gossiping this way?"

My hand stilled with the coffee cup halfway to my mouth. "I hadn't thought of it as gossiping. I thought we were solving a murder."

"True." Mom shrugged. "But after this, I need to find a way to curtail the information the craft ladies give me. I don't care to know everyone's dirty laundry."

Neither did I, but in this case, it seemed a necessary evil. "We still have plenty of suspects. Does anyone in particular stand out in your mind?"

"Mr. Dean moved his secret affections from Mrs. Grimes to Estelle Willis pretty quick. Doesn't make him a killer, though, just cold-hearted."

"I gave him the antique books yesterday. From Mrs. Grimes's journal, it was plain to see she cared about him. Why would he kill her though? It wasn't as if the information of their relationship would affect anyone if it became common knowledge."

"I thought he was your top choice."

"He was. Now, I'm not so sure." It was just a feeling I had, but the pain in the man's eyes when I'd given him the books haunted me. There had to be a reason they'd kept their love a secret. "Mrs. Willis is writing a book that parallel's the murders. She's my top choice now."

"It's possible she wrote the chapters after hearing the details."

"Maybe. I still think it warrants a conversation with her." Now to find a way to bring up the subject without the woman knowing I'd read her manuscript. "We'd better get to work." I also needed to find time to separate the latest fliers into stacks of thirty and staple a flier of the fair activities to each page. The days weren't long enough for everything I needed to do.

Although I was bound to love whatever Duane came up with for our honeymoon, I prayed it was something that took us away from here for at least a week. No more murders or mysteries for me.

"Why don't you take the time to go see Mrs. Willis and I'll open the store?" Mom said. "You'll be back before any rush."

"Today's the day the women from the retirement center go shopping."

"They don't come until ten." Mom took my mug and set mine and hers in the sink. "I'll be fine until then."

"Okay." Maybe I'd find something to say to the woman by the time I arrived at the school. It was time to light a fire under the rear end of each suspect. The thought gave me chills.

While Mom headed toward the store, I headed for the school, pulling into the lot as Duane got out of his truck. The sight of him brightened my day, and I honked.

He turned with a grin and met me half-way across the parking lot. "Hey, beautiful."

"Hey, handsome." I lifted my face for a kiss. "Careful. We might get busted for PDA and have to spend a day in detention."

He cradled my face in his hands. "I'm willing to take that chance." He kissed me long and thorough before pulling back. "What are you up to?"

I explained about the manuscript. He frowned as I talked. "I guess you'll be safe here at the school, but then I want you to head straight to the store. I don't want you or Gertie to be alone at any time. Understood?"

"Yes, and I'm in total agreement. I'd stop all this if I could."

He nodded. "I know, but you're in too deep now. It shouldn't be too hard to find a way to bring up the subject of her book. Everyone knows she's writing one." He glanced at his watch. "She has prep first hour. You can probably catch her in the teacher's lounge."

"Thanks." We walked into the school together, then parted ways. I tossed a wave to Cheryl, now in the small office manager's office. She already looked more harried than usual.

As Duane thought, Estelle was in the lounge, her laptop open on the table. I pretended to be busy studying the teacher's cubbies. I should have thought to bring something with me to look like work. As it was, it was obvious I was hovering.

"Did you want something?" Estelle sighed. "You're making it hard for me to concentrate."

"Actually, yes." I pulled out a chair and sat across from her. "I'm thinking of writing a book, and you're the first person I thought of."

She snorted. "Everyone wants to be a writer. Go ahead, ask your questions."

"What genre are you writing?"

"Murder mystery."

"Where do you get your ideas?" No sense in beating around the bush.

"From life." She crossed her arms. "Somehow, I get the feeling you already know all this."

"Some of it." No point in lying. If Estelle is the killer, she already knows what I know. I bit my bottom lip. How could I bring up the subject of Mrs. Grimes and Stacy? "What sort of research do you do? I mean, if you have someone stab someone, how would you know what it was really like unless you'd actually stabbed someone?"

"There are ways around that, Marsha. You're still as nosy as you were as a child." She pointed a finger at me. "Sometimes, that can get you in a lot of trouble."

"Is that a warning?"

"It's advice." Her eyes narrowed. "You think I killed Harriet and that reporter, don't you?" She cackled. "Oh, this is priceless. I may just have to put it in my next book. Nosy mom accuses upstanding teacher of murder."

"Did you?" I leaned my elbows on the table and speared her with the most intense look I could muster. "I've seen your manuscript." I held up a hand as she started to speak. "It doesn't matter how I got a hold of it. The details are pretty accurate for someone to have read about the crimes in the paper. I gave the manuscript to the police." Satisfied, I straightened.

Her eyes widened. "You've ruined me. If word gets out…" She shook her head. "Meddlesome, that's what you are. One of these days, your luck will run out, and I'll write about it in a novel."

"Is that a threat?"

"It's a promise." She leaned across the table until our noses were inches apart. "I've never liked you Marsha Callahan. Not even when I was your teacher. Don't bother writing a book. You're skills aren't up to par."

"It's Marsha Steele."

"Whatever. Go stick your nose in someone else's business." She sat back down and started typing. "We're done here."

I shoved away from the table. The conversation could have gone either way, I suppose. I didn't expect her to confess, but she gave me enough information to keep her at the top of my suspect list. If she was the killer, maybe she'd make her move soon and this whole thing would be over. As long as over didn't mean me lying on a slab in the funeral home.

On my way out of the lounge, I passed Mr. Dean. He avoided my gaze, but his landed on Estelle instead. Her eyes flickered toward him before returning to her computer screen. If the two were in a relationship, things were on the rocks.

I headed to the front office and marched up to Cheryl's desk. "Congratulations on the promotion."

Her eyes filled with tears. "Everyone thinks I got Sarah fired on purpose so I could have her job. I didn't! All I did was inform Mr. Dean that she hadn't booked the buses for the third grade field trip. Since it wasn't the first time, he reported her to the board. Then, she told him she had a cruise booked for December. When he denied her request because of the time frame, she ordered the tickets anyway."

"I doubt it was your fault. It's not that easy to get fired from a school unless you're into something illegal or immoral." Most likely it was the purchasing of the tickets when she'd been told no. Even I knew that working right before the Christmas break was mandatory. What was wrong with people?

River Valley seemed to be overrun with strangers. What happened to our peaceful little town? Crime used to be virtually nonexistent. Now, there was a murder every six months. And it all started with the women's ministry at the church when the leader wanted to adopt a child from South America.

That one act seemed to have opened Pandora's Box, and I was getting sucked into the vortex.

19

"Mom?" Lindsey entered the kitchen, her face creased with worry. Behind her marched Officer Bradford.

I slid my notes under the morning paper. "Officer. Can we help you? Would you like a cup of coffee?"

"This isn't a social call, Mrs. Steele." He squared his shoulders. "We received an anonymous call to the station alerting us to the fact that you killed Mrs. Grimes."

"What?" I shot to my feet, spilling my coffee over the newspaper. "That's ridiculous. What possible motive would I have? Where's Bruce?"

"Officer Barnett is following other leads."

I glanced over his shoulder at my daughter. "Lindsey, go to school. Everything is fine here."

"But—"

"Go to school." My neck heated. This latest killer was a coward, accusing innocent people of their devious crimes. Well, I wouldn't stand for it. Not for a minute.

Once Lindsey scooted out the door, I turned

back to the officer who didn't look much older than my daughter. "What did the anonymous caller say?"

"That if we search your house, we'll find evidence that you killed both victims." He glanced toward the knife block on the counter.

My gaze followed his. One of the knives was missing. How could I not have noticed that before? It must have happened during our break-in. "If you think one of my knives was used to kill Stacy, you're wrong. It wasn't the same brand." The one that had stuck out of Stacy's chest had had a red handle. I was certain of it. Mine were stainless steel.

"Perhaps." He looked taken aback that I knew such a detail from the crime. Most likely, that was a fact they wanted kept secret in order to whittle the killer out of the list of suspects. "That particular weapon is easily found at Wal-Mart."

"Then why the interest in the empty spot in my knife block?" I crossed my arms. "This is harassment, plain and simple, and a clear tactic to throw y'all off the real killer's tracks. It appears to be working." If they didn't get their heads on straight and catch this person, one of my family might be the next victim, and that was something I would not stand back and let happen.

"What's going on?" Mom entered through the back door, clearly arriving for her morning coffee chat with me.

"Officer Bradford seems to think that since we're missing a knife, that I killed Stacy."

"That's ridiculous. Besides, I borrowed the knife yesterday to chop carrots. It's at the cottage." She poured herself a cup of coffee, and then noticed my spill on the table. She sighed and grabbed a rag.

She grabbed the sodden papers from the table, my notes included, and dumped the lot in the trash. I could fish the notes out later, when Office Sharp Eyes wasn't around. First Bruce kept his nose in my business, now this upstart. The day hadn't started well and would most likely go downhill from here.

"Now, unless you plan to arrest me," I said. "I'm going to ask you to leave. Does Bruce know you're here?"

"No, ma'am, he doesn't. I don't need to clear my actions with him."

"Be sure that I will tell him of your visit. Good day." I marched to the front door and held it open. "If you actually find incriminating evidence against me, feel free to return. I've enjoyed our visit."

He rolled his eyes and left. I closed the door and sagged against the painted wood. I had an hour until my dress fitting. This ugly accusation threatened to ruin the joy of the day.

"Our killer has to be a woman," Mom said from the kitchen doorway. "Only women are this sneaky."

"Maybe." I grabbed my purse. "I've got to go or I'll miss my fitting. The suspect notes were under the newspaper. Could you see whether they are salvageable?"

"Yep. I'll see you at the store in a couple of hours."

While I drove, my mind circled around what facts I knew. One…someone needed money bad enough to kill for something that might or might not exist. Two…I was closer than I thought or they wouldn't be taking such drastic measures as trying to cast suspicion on me. Three…well, other than a list of suspects that might or might not contain the actual killer, I had nothing else.

I drove past Norma Rae's tea room where she and her daughter yelled at each other on the sidewalk. What was up with those two? If I weren't so focused on the case at hand, I might do a bit of nosing around there. Maybe I'd stop at the tea room on my way back into town. Both women stopped screaming as I passed, and I watched them through the rearview mirror. Neither of them turned away.

From a side street, a police cruiser pulled onto the main road. Officer Bradford, no doubt. Well, he could follow me for the next thirty miles and be the first to catch a glimpse of my wedding dress. Idiot. With a grin on my face, I circled around, leading the officer on a winding route to our destination. I might arrive at my fitting a few minutes later, but I'd feel better about the morning.

When I arrived at the dress shop, I exited the car and tossed a jaunty wave at Officer Bradford as he sped by. He must not think my destination was interesting after all. The good thing about him following me…the killer couldn't get close enough to cause me harm.

I pushed through the double glass doors and approached the counter. A few minutes later, the sales girl brought me the one dress in the world that made me feel like a princess. She helped me into the gown, made the minor adjustments with clips, and I was back behind the wheel of the jeep. After glancing around to see whether I still had an escort, and not seeing one, I pulled back onto the highway and headed back to River Valley.

A closed sign on the door of the tea room kept me continuing to Country Gifts from Heaven. Asking Norma Rae more questions would have to wait.

I parked in the alley behind the store. I turned the knob on the back door and pushed. It was locked. "Mom?" I pounded before peering through the slit of a window.

"Sorry," she said after unlocking the door and letting me in. "A person can't be too careful nowadays."

"True." I set my purse in the cupboard and moved to the front of the store.

Norma Rae stood on the other side of the counter. In front of her was a cardboard box. "I've come to sell a few things on consignment. These are antique tea cups and saucers. I believe they'll catch a good price."

I glanced in the box and caught my breath. "They're exquisite. Are some of them trimmed in real gold?"

She shrugged. "Maybe."

"But don't you use these in your shop?"

"I'm closing the tea room. There isn't enough business to make a profit. I know of another way to make money."

Mom started setting the delicate china cups on the counter. "I heard you'd have to move in with your daughter."

"I'll avoid that at all costs."

"What is between you two, if you don't mind

my asking?" I held up a delicate white cup with tiny blue flowers. "Y'all's relationship seems a bit…strained. Maybe Mom and I can help. We have a great relationship."

"Well, aren't you lucky?" Norma Rae smirked. "Not everyone gets along with their children. If they did, we wouldn't have the amount of child abuse that is so prevalent in our society. Do you want the cups or not?"

"Definitely." I set the one I held with the others. "We keep twenty percent of what they sell for. Have you had them appraised? If not, we can find someone for you."

"Just sell them." Norma whirled and marched from the store.

"That is one unhappy woman." Mom pulled a sheet of paper from under the counter and started cataloguing the cups. "Did you get a glimpse of her shoes?"

"No, why?" I dashed to the front door.

"She had on ballet flats."

"So, I'm wearing ballet flats." I went outside and searched the surrounding area for a footprint. There, next to a puddle of water was a rapidly drying imprint of a smooth soled shoe. I rushed back inside. "How did you notice that?"

"Before you arrived, she sat in the rocker and removed a pebble from her shoe." Mom grinned. "Am I a good spy or what?"

"You're the best!" Now, what could I do with the information? Bruce would only laugh and tell me Norma Rae wasn't the only woman in town wearing those types of shoes. He would be right.

But, since she was already a suspect, maybe he'd pay attention.

I grabbed the phone off the counter and dialed his private number. "Bruce?"

"Hello, Marsha."

"Did you know that Officer Bradford received a call this morning about me being the killer? He came to the house and practically accused me."

"He was only checking out a lead."

"So, you did know."

"He called me a few minutes ago. What do you want? I'm busy."

I plopped into the nearest rocking chair. "Are you following a lead?"

"I can't divulge that information."

Yeah, yeah. "I have another one for you."

"Do tell." His sigh was so heavy I could almost feel his breath over the phone line.

"Norma Rae Jenning's is wearing shoes that match the print we found." I closed my eyes and waited.

"Do you know how many women in River Valley wear those shoes? At least twenty. I've been counting. That means nothing. I've told you to stay out this, Marsha. What will it take for you to follow my orders?"

For him to catch the murderer, but somehow I didn't think he'd appreciate that answer. "I'm doing my best—"

Mom grabbed the phone out of my hand. "Bruce Barnett! Your mother is rolling in her grave right now, upset at the way you must be talking to my daughter. Yes, I can imagine. I can see the stricken look on her face. If you'd get off your rear end and catch this crazy person, Marsha and I wouldn't have to." She slammed the receiver on the hook.

"Stricken, Mom?" Really, I doubted I had any such look on my face.

"I'm playing the Irish mom guilt trip," she said. "Hopefully, it will work."

I shrugged and moved to the computer to find an appraiser for the tea cups. Norma Rae wouldn't make enough to save her business or even to prevent her from moving in with Ingrid, but it would be something to offset some of her costs.

The relationship between the two Jennings women tore at my heart. I glanced at Mom. How would it feel to dislike your mother so much? Or for Mom to virtually hate me? I couldn't fathom it. Lindsey might cop a teenage attitude sometimes, but the girl loved me. Of that I had no doubt.

I found a prospective appraiser and sent an email. Since I had to count out fliers and do some stapling, Mom grabbed a crocheted table runner and started working. Most of the time, I did the crafts and she worked the counter, and I deeply appreciated her willingness to switch roles for the day. I hoped someone slapped me the next time I volunteered for something while in the middle of a mystery.

Wait. What was I saying? I would never, ever, get involved in another mystery. My nerves couldn't take it. I'd get through the book fair and this investigation and focus on married life with Duane. Then, the most pressing question that would need answered was whether I wanted another child

or not.
Sometimes, that question scared me the most.

20

Who was the crazy person that scheduled the book club and the PTO meeting on the same night? The club meeting is scheduled for six and the PTO for seven. I shoved a handful of M&Ms into my mouth. With all the stress swirling around me, and my tendency to turn to chocolate, I'd be lucky to fit into my wedding dress in two months.

To compensate, I skipped supper since Lindsey was studying at a friend's house anyway and rushed to the cottage to fetch Mom. I wasn't facing the Piranhas alone.

She met me in the yard. "I'm coming. Can't a girl get a bite to eat before rushing out the door? It isn't good for the digestion."

"We've a full schedule tonight." I hurried to my jeep. Mom opened her Cadillac. I sighed and joined her. I had no energy to argue with her about who was driving.

I slid into the passenger seat and buckled my seatbelt. Mom had a tendency to treat her car as if she were driving in a NASCAR race.

"Relax." She turned the key in the ignition. "I'll

get us there in one piece."

We arrived at the church for the book club meeting ten minutes late, despite Mom's speedy driving. She slammed on the brakes in front of the fellowship hall and we sprinted inside. Estelle was new face in the group. She glanced up and gave a snide smile. In front of each seat was a pile of papers. Her manuscript.

"The book club has decided to give me valuable feedback," she said. "Since you somehow already read it, I guess you don't need a fresh copy."

I rolled my eyes and took a seat as far from her as I could, which wasn't far considering we sat at a round table. "Mom hasn't read it."

Estelle handed Mom a copy. "How is your book coming, Marsha?" She glanced around the group. "Did you ladies know she was writing one of her own?"

I'd forgotten the little white lie I'd told. All eyes turned in my direction.

"What's your book about, Marsha?" Cheryl asked. "If we would have known, we could have brainstormed with you."

"I, uh, thought I'd write about the mysteries I've been involved in. Make it a series of sorts." Good grief. I couldn't write a book to save my life.

"Well, don't use Harriet's death." Estelle tapped the manuscript in front of her. "I've already used it."

Tears welled in Cheryl's eyes. "Somehow that seems so disrespectful to our dear friend."

"She was no friend of mine," Estelle said. "I have no qualms writing about her death."

I'm sure she didn't, the evil witch.

"Well," Norma Rae crossed her arms and glowered across the table at Ingrid. "If anyone wants to know what it feels like to want to kill someone, just ask me. I'll be a great research source."

"Oh, stuff it, Mother." Ingrid grabbed her purse. "This club is a ridiculous waste of time. Consider me resigned." She marched out the door without a backward glance.

Norma Rae pointed at the door. "See my point? The girl is hopeless."

"If you weren't so mean to her, she might not be." Mom straightened her shoulders. "I would never dream of talking to Marsha the way you talk to Ingrid."

"You don't know a thing about it, you Nosey Nellie!" Norma Rae shoved back her chair. "You and your perfect little life. And you, Estelle, can shove your stupid book where the sun doesn't shine!" She stormed out of the room.

"Well!" Estelle gathered up the copies of her manuscript. "If this is how you ladies run this book club, I want nothing to do with any of it. I have another meeting to attend anyway." She followed the other two, leaving me, Mom, and Cheryl staring at each other.

"I guess the meeting is adjourned." Cheryl picked up her purse from the floor at her feet.

"Sweetie," Mom said. "I'd say the club is disbanded."

Cheryl shrugged. "Well, I have a lot on my plate right now. It's just as well. See the two of you at the

PTSO meeting."

Why did I keep forgetting they'd added the S into the PTO? "Mom, I'm starving. Can we grab a burger before heading to the school?"

"Sure thing." We left the building, turning the lights off behind us.

What a strange twenty minutes. I couldn't say I'd miss the club since I only joined to try and dig up information on Mrs. Grimes's death, but it was an interesting time for sure. I thanked God for relieving the item from my stress-filled plate and got into Mom's boat of a car.

After stopping for a burger and fries, we arrived at the school a few minutes early. I carried my supper into the library with me. I sighed. The new librarian had already set up the book fair tables and books. No decorations were threaded throughout the items for sale. Nothing showed that there would be a carnival of sorts in a few days. I still had a lot of work ahead of me.

The attendees for tonight's meeting were small, consisting of me and Mom, Mr. Dean, Cheryl, Estelle, and the Snyders. I supposed that Sarah Boatwright no longer wanted to attend due to being fired as office manager. To my surprise and delight, Duane waltzed in moments after Mom and me.

I grinned and motioned to the seat next to me. "This is a surprise."

"I figured since this meeting is about the fair, I might as well attend and let everyone know how the main attraction is progressing." He glanced around the room. "I thought there'd be some decorations in here."

"I guess that's up to me."

"I'll handle this," Mom said. "I've plenty of plastic pumpkins and greenery to spruce this place up before the big night."

"We've already had a few sales," Cheryl said. "If everyone will take their seats, we can get started. The sooner we do, the sooner everyone can head home."

Sounded good to me. I gave her my utmost attention.

"First up," Cheryl glanced at her notes, "is Marsha Steele. Marsha, please fill us in on the progress."

I hadn't known I'd have to speak. My mouth filled with cotton. "Well, everything is looking good. All jobs are filled, fliers in teacher's boxes, and Duane is working on the tunnel along with my stepfather, Leroy Bohan. We have plenty of student council members to work the haunted tunnel and each class is doing a booth of some kind. I'm confident it will be a wonderful night for the school." I exhaled sharply and sat back in my seat.

"Coach? How is the tunnel coming along?" Cheryl motioned for Duane to speak.

"It's almost ready. We'll set it up the night before, and Officer Barnett has promised police coverage for the night."

Cheryl's eyes widened. "Is that necessary?"

"We don't want any students goofing off any more than usual," Duane said. "It's only a precaution. There will be a lot going on that night. Extra eyes will be appreciated. I've also commissioned the football team to help with clean up."

"That's wonderful." Cheryl cast him an appreciative look. "I don't think we've thought of clean up." She frowned at me.

Hey, I didn't ask for all the responsibility. Only some of it.

"Mr. Dean, do you have anything to add?" Cheryl asked.

He raised red-rimmed eyes. "No. Look's like it's all taken care of. You've done a good job."

She beamed under his praise. Estelle huffed. Surely the elderly teacher wasn't jealous of Cheryl? She was young enough to be Mr. Dean's daughter.

A closer watch of the wanna-be author might be in store. Especially if Cheryl appeared to be in any trouble. We didn't need any more deaths in the name of research.

Mom dropped a pencil and spent a lot of time under the table looking for it. I yanked on her shirt tail. "What are you doing?"

"Looking at people's shoes. Why else would I bother coming to this meeting if not to squeeze in some sleuthing."

"Well?"

"Cheryl is wearing flats, but I can't see the soles. Same with Estelle and Janet Snyder. What happened to women wearing heels?"

"Flats are in style and more comfortable." I studied the Snyders. They'd remained quiet during the entire meeting so far and if their body language was any indication, the two were having a silent dispute. I didn't really consider either of them a major suspect, though, so left them to their disagreement.

When the meeting's agenda moved away from the fair, I mulled over my two main suspects...Norma Rae and Estelle. I found it hard to believe that either of them could kill a young, strong woman like Stacy, but I couldn't rule out the possibility.

Norma Rae carried a lot of anger inside her skinny body, while Estelle seemed focused on getting her book published no matter what. I might be grasping at straws, but they seemed the most likely ones to have killed Mrs. Grimes. In my mind at least. I just needed that elusive concrete evidence.

"A penny for your thoughts." Duane's breath tickled my ear.

"Rounding up suspects."

"I figured as much. Who do you suspect?"

"Norma Rae Jennings and Estelle Willis."

He raised his eyebrows. "Let's get out of here while you tell me why. Maybe I can shed some light over ice cream."

I whispered to Mom that we were leaving and the three of us slipped out of the meeting like fugitives. Mom and I followed Duane to the local Dairy Queen and sat in the booth we'd sat in shortly after Duane's arrival back in River Valley. Had that really been less than a year? We'd sat in that very booth and watched out the window while a killer stalked my daughter.

While we waited for our ice cream, I filled Duane in on why I'd chosen those two ladies as my main suspects.

"It does seem suspicious that Estelle knows so

much about the murders," he said. "But that doesn't make her a killer. Norma Rae, well, I don't know enough about her to make a judgment. She does seem very unhappy."

"Could you maybe use your charm on Ingrid and find out why she and her mother hate each other so much?"

"My charm?"

"Yeah. Ingrid seems lonely. Attention from a handsome man—"

"You want to pimp me out?" A dimple winked from beside his mouth.

"That's a great idea," Mom said. "I'd have Leroy do it, but you're more Ingrid's age."

Duane laughed. "You two beat all, you know that? I am not going to flirt with a woman just to garner information from her."

"Why not?" I called after him as he moved to get our ice cream. "It happens all the time in one way or another." At least in the movies. Why wouldn't it work in real life?

He slid back into the booth. "I can't start talking to a woman I've never officially met and dig for information. It won't work. I'll focus on Estelle. We have the same lunch time."

I'd take what help I could get. "Just don't be alone with her. If she is the killer…I don't want to lose you."

"I think I can handle a sixty-year-old woman."

I took a bite of my sundae. I felt pretty good about having narrowed my suspect list down to two. Hopefully, the right two. If only Bruce would be more forthcoming with his own information.

Supposedly, he'd been actively investigating the case. I was sure he was having help from the marshal's office. After all, there were two victims now.

Somehow, I needed to find out what he knew. The only person that could possibly get me the information didn't seem to like me much. Still, I'd pay Ingrid a visit and invite her to lunch.

21

"Good morning, Ingrid." I leaned over the receptionist desk at the police station. "How's the hand?"

She glared at me over her glasses. "Officer Barnett isn't in, and the hand is fine, thank you."

"I'm actually here to see you." How did someone ask someone to lunch who clearly disliked the person doing the asking?

"Oh, really?" She straightened in her chair and crossed her arms. "Want more information on mine and mom's storming out of the book club? Or is there something more sinister on your mind?"

"Why would I have something sinister on my mind?" Really. The woman didn't know me well enough to make such an assumption.

She gave a sinister smile. "Are you digging for any information I might have overheard regarding the death of Mrs. Grimes and Miss Tate?"

"Possibly." I grinned. "Are you up to it?"

She shrugged. "Sure, I'll bite." She grabbed her purse. "The fact that Mother will be livid at finding out I had lunch with you is enough to make the idea sound good to me. Let's go."

If Ingrid wanted our lunch date to be common

knowledge, there was no better place than Wanda's Diner. We strolled in like best friends, arms linked together, and took a booth in the back. Wanda raised eyebrows at the sight of us and several other customers took second glances. What in the world was so strange about us eating together?

"Is your mother talking about me?" I asked the moment we sat and had menus in front of us. "We seem to be attracting more attention than I thought we would."

"She's complaining about you all over town." Ingrid smiled more at that statement than the whole time I'd known her. Actually, it might be the only time I've seen her smile.

I squirmed in my seat. Maybe having lunch with her wasn't such a good idea. But what could possibly go wrong in a crowded diner? Any sinister business and Wanda would be on the phone with Bruce in an instant.

"What is she saying?" I folded my menu and set it aside, deciding on a salad.

"That you're harassing her, slandering her good name, turning people away from her tea shop." As I opened my mouth to protest, she held up a hand. "I know you aren't doing those things, but Mother is upset at having to live with me. I have to admit to a certain amount of misgiving at the idea myself. In case you haven't noticed, we don't exactly get along. But, I've found a way out of my predicament."

Lindsey approached to take our orders, a questioning look blanketing her face. "May I take your orders?"

"Why aren't you in school? This job takes second place, young lady."

"It's early release day so Wanda said I could come in early. Seriously, Mom, you need to pay better attention to my schedule." Her pencil poised over her order pad.

"Sorry. I'll take the chef's salad, ranch dressing, please."

"I'll have the same." Ingrid handed Lindsey our menus. "Lovely girl," she said, after Lindsey left. "You're lucky to have such a good relationship with her." Sadness clouded her eyes. "So, what is it you want to know?"

"Does Bruce have any suspects?" I pulled a small spiral notebook out of my purse and fished for a pen.

"Of course he does. The man is brilliant in his field."

Uh-oh. "You have a crush on him?"

"Don't be silly. I'm marrying Officer Wilson."

"But he's old enough to be your father." I clapped a hand over my mouth. "Sorry."

"He's good to me. That's all that matters."

"That's your plan to escape living with your mother?"

"Yes." She grinned again. "Oscar has already agreed not to give in to her complaints."

Wow. The world was full of surprises. "Do you know who the suspects are?"

She glanced around the room. "The book club members, the PTSO, you."

"Me? Bruce knows me better than that. We've known each other since Kindergarten."

"But Officer Bradford hasn't. He says he doesn't trust you. That maybe you enjoy the notoriety of solving crimes before the police."

"That doesn't make any sense. If I killed in order to solve the crime, I'd have to accuse myself." The man might be handsome, but he was clearly an idiot.

"I'm just telling you what he says. Of course, Officer Barnett is too clever to believe him." She waited until Lindsey brought us our salads and left before continuing. "A word of warning, dear Marsha…if you don't stop nosing around, Officer Barnett is going to arrest you."

"He's said that before."

"I think he's serious this time."

I stabbed a piece of hard-boiled egg with my fork. "Have you heard anything else? Anything that will help me, or the police, put a stop to these murders? Maybe you've heard something that didn't mean much at the time you heard it. Maybe something about the footprint found outside my shop?"

She sat in thought for a moment, her face paling. "No, can't say as I have."

She was lying. I knew it as sure as the salad in front of me. I forked a cherry tomato into my mouth. I could ask her what she knew, but since she didn't volunteer the information, even going as far as saying she didn't know anything, I doubted I'd get any more out of her. We sat in silence, the clank of our silverware against the plates seeming to echo. On pretense of studying her shoes, I dropped my napkin. There was no way her size tens made the print. I was no closer to new clues than I was that morning.

After we finished eating, I paid the bill, left Lindsey a five dollar tip, and followed Ingrid back to my jeep. I pulled in front of the police station. "Thank you for joining me."

"I'm sorry I wasn't more help."

"That's all right. It was worth a shot."

"I hope we can do this again sometime." She opened the door. "I don't have many friends, thanks to my mother."

"Sure, we can."

"And, Marsha." She stepped outside and closed the door, sticking her head back through the open window. "Please be careful. The person you're dealing with is evil personified." With those encouraging words, she marched into the building.

She did know who the killer was! I sped to Country Gifts from Heaven. I couldn't wait to share the news with Mom.

When I arrived, the store was full of customers buying fall themed decorations. I kept busy restocking shelves as items were purchased, all the while impatient for them to leave. From the back of the store came the excited chatter of the craft group. I'd forgotten they'd booked the room that day. No matter. They often had valuable input.

After the rush of customers had subsided, I sat at the crafting table where the women were making Thanksgiving centerpieces for the retirement home. The talent of the ladies never failed to astound me. Maybe Mom and I should make a few to sell in the store.

"Ladies, I need your help."

As one they set down their work and stared. "Let's have it," Betty said.

I told them of my lunch with Ingrid and her peculiar behavior when I mentioned the footprint. "I'm certain she knows who the killer is."

"It sure seems like it," Dottie said. "But that quiet girl will never tell. She'd never put herself in jeopardy the way you do."

"Did y'all know she's marrying Officer Wilson?" I poked loose needles into a pincushion.

"Well, he isn't the murderer," Betty said. The three Bates sisters nodded. "He has no motive."

True. I rubbed the beginning of a headache from my temples. "Do you think it's the new officer?"

"Bradford?" Mom shook her head, leaning against the counter. "I doubt it, although the man is a nuisance. Came into the store again this morning to talk to you. I told him I'd pass on the information. There. I did. What you do with it is up to you. Oh, and I found a buyer for Norma Rae's tea cups. A thousand dollars for the lot. A nice little profit. Norma Rae should be here any time for her check."

"How's the fair coming along?" Betty asked. "Aren't you afraid of having a lot of folks in scary costumes considering all that is going on?"

"I've considered the danger." More than I'd like to, if I were honest. The fact I'd have to stick close to the haunted tunnel in order to make sure things ran smoothly terrified me. I still couldn't get the image of someone with a real knife chasing me out of my head. The only consolation was that Duane would be a part of things and that Bruce and the other officers would be on hand. Of course, if Officer Bradford thought me the guilty party, he might not be too inclined to protect me. Maybe, his suspicions about me would keep him close.

"Hello?" Norma Rae peered around the corner. "What's this? Doesn't anyone work around here anymore?"

"This is a craft group," Betty explained. "And we're all amateur detectives. We're helping Marsha find a killer. We don't have time for nonsense."

I cringed. Betty had just told a prime suspect that we were brainstorming the murders. "I'll help you, Norma Rae." I leaped from my chair and followed her back to the front of the store. "We owe you eight hundred dollars. Not a bad little profit for you."

"Not nearly enough." She placed her purse on the counter, the bag making a clunk against the Formica top. "I heard you had lunch with Ingrid today. I'm warning you to stay out of my business, Marsha. I'm not afraid of filing a complaint against you."

"There's nothing against the law about having lunch with a friend." I pulled the checkbook from the counter safe.

"Ingrid doesn't have any friends, and she doesn't need any like you."

"She's an adult. She can make up her own mind about who she makes friends with." I should have let mother wait on the woman. I wrote out the check, ripped it from the book, and then slid it across the counter to her. "Have a good day."

"This isn't over. Not by a long shot." She snatched the check and marched from the store.

How could someone be so unhappy? I sent a prayer heavenward for the woman and joined the others again.

"I'm sorry." Tears shimmered in Betty's eyes. "Gertie told me that she was one of your suspects, and I've gone and opened my big mouth."

"It's all right." The fair started tomorrow night. Things could very well be over soon. Either the killer would get me or I'd get them. Either way, there would be no more sleepless nights or watching my rearview mirror every time I drove somewhere.

Soon, the women gathered up their supplies and left. Mom and I cleaned up the store and headed out, her to fix Leroy his supper, and me to the school to oversee the setting up of the fair exhibits.

I sent Duane a text when I'd arrived at the football field and he met me in the parking lot. "The skeleton of the tunnel is set up from the side of the snack bar all the way to the side entrance of the library. It will take the students a good ten to fifteen minutes to walk through it. Less if they run." He grinned and put an arm around my shoulder. "Leroy did a great job building it. We've hung the black lights inside and are now covering it with the black plastic sheeting. You had a good idea, sweetheart. That's all the kids have been talking about all day."

I stopped and stared at the winding tunnel. It strongly resembled a giant anaconda. As long as it didn't swallow anyone whole, we'd all be okay.

22

The football field was full of folks eager to spend their hard-earned cash on some harvest fun. Little ones, dressed in Halloween finery, giggled and tossed rings at bowls of gold fish. Several girls walked in a circle to music hoping to win a cake. The line outside the haunted tunnel was fifty or more deep with students. I spotted a couple of adults in the mix. I rubbed my hands together. The school and library would make a bundle of money.

I hadn't seen any member of my family since arriving but trusted they were all in their spots. Except, Lindsey. I'd allowed her some fun time with friends. She was going to be the first to enter the tunnel, and hopefully report back on how wonderful it was.

After waving to Cheryl who took tickets at the gate, I made my way to the library. Mom had outdone herself with fall decorations. Pumpkins and gold and orange flowers covered every available surface. Parents with children of all ages browsed the tables and book stands. A grin spread across my face erasing the tension of the past few weeks. I'd done it. I'd fulfilled the wish of a woman I barely knew and delivered a book fair the school wouldn't forget.

I followed the screams to the exit of the tunnel and waited for Lindsey. She appeared, arms around her friend. They were both pale faced but smiling.

"That was a blast, Mom. So much fun. And so scary!" She shuddered. "The maniacs from all the slash and gore movies are in there. I swear the one acts just like Michael Meyers, and the zombies!"

"I'm glad you had fun. Can you let everyone you know how much fun it is?" With the tunnel taking five tickets, it was the most expensive attraction we had.

"I'm sure they already know. Have you seen the line?" She gave me a quick hug and dashed outside.

Curiosity rose, but I squelched it. I didn't do scary things. Well, unless you counted facing down the barrel of a gun as I had twice, but that wasn't by my choosing. I wandered the football field. Several of the teachers complimented me on a job well done and said they hoped I'd head up the fair again next year. I wasn't sure about that, but smiled and waved anyway enjoying my moment of fame that didn't involve almost getting myself killed.

Officer Bradford emerged from the crowd and made a beeline in my direction. I thought about trying to lose him in the crowd and decided against it. If a policeman followed me around, it would be harder for a killer to get close. "Enjoying yourself, Officer?"

"I'm not here for recreation."

"I guess not. You're here to watch me. Well,

I'm working, so keep up." I marched toward the climbing wall run by a couple of football players who didn't want to participate in the tunnel.

"Coach isn't here, Mrs. Coach," one of them said. "He's pretending to be Freddy Krueger. You should see his makeup. It's awesome."

I shuddered. I didn't last through the first ten minutes of that movie and no desire to recreate the experience. The boys seemed to have all the safety measures in place for the kids climbing the wall so I moved back to the entrance of the tunnel. I pictured all the anxious grins fading to terrified expressions as they moved through. From the screams pouring out the entrance, the tunnel was a place of nightmares. I peeked inside.

A shuffling zombie gnashed its teeth at a teenage girl. She screamed and dashed away, disappearing around a dark corner. Maybe I should venture inside. After all, I was an adult and it was only for a bit of fun, right?

The young man taking tickets waved me in. I took a deep breath, waved at Officer Bradford, and then dashed inside to stay as close to one side of the tunnel as I could get. As far away from the zombie's reach as possible. When I rounded the corner, Freddy Krueger wrapped his taloned hands around my shoulders. I shrieked and beat him off. "Stop it, Duane! You'll give me a heart attack."

"Don't fall asleep, my beauty," he whispered. "Enjoy the tour."

"Very funny." I was already regretting my impulsive decision.

I stopped and watched as a lab-coated football

player operated on a girl with her intestines spilling out. How did anyone find this entertaining? I grimaced and moved on. The next section was almost pitch dark. Filmy things hung from the ceiling and tickled my face like cobwebs. Ugh. I slapped them away.

A scream close to my left caused me to whirl, bringing me face-to-face with Michael Meyers. He raised his knife. I dashed down the tunnel and came into a small room full of coffins.

A vampire sat up and gave me the corny line about wanting to suck my blood. I shook my head and continued on past three witches stirring something in a cauldron. Before I took another step one of them rushed me, her pointed nails clawing the air. I backed up and fell through the plastic sheeting that made up the tunnel sides.

Call me a scaredy-cat but I was happy to be out of the tunnel of horror. I was in a small room with a table and four chairs. A small gas-powered refrigerator sat at one end of the tiny room. I opened it and pulled out a bottle of water. I didn't see a door. I'd have to go back into the fun in order to leave. After downing half the bottle, I pushed back into the tunnel.

A sharp rap to the back of my head sent me to my knees. A person wearing all black with a faceless mask grasped my ankles. I kicked and freed myself. Before I could struggle to my feet, the person jumped on my back, wrapping their legs around me. Black ballet flats pressed into my abdomen. I knew those shoes.

"Norma Rae, get off me!" I rammed my head

back, connecting with something solid. I hoped I'd managed to break her nose. I turned, my back against a plaster mummy. "Officer Bradford is expecting me at any minute. You should turn yourself in."

She shook her head and pulled a knife out of a hidden pocket before advancing on me again. I skirted to the side. "You're such an idiot, Marsha. This is all part of the fun. Run back to your bodyguard."

"I will." I whirled and sprinted away. My breath came in gasps. Was she part of the act or had the knife been real? I had no way of knowing. If it was part of her character, someone needed to tell her that she wasn't actually allowed to touch any of the people visiting the tunnel. Imagine the lawsuit if someone were to get hurt.

I brushed off the knees of my jeans and rushed through the rest of the tour. Outside, I gulped in a lungful of fresh air.

"Everything all right?" Officer Bradford appeared at my side. "You look like you've been in a fight."

"Depends on what you call a fight." I straightened. "Don't you have anything better to do than follow me around? Like make sure the students are behaving?"

"I was told to watch you."

"By Bruce?"

He nodded. "It seems he thinks someone needs to keep an eye on you. Probably to keep you from causing trouble."

I shook my head. The poor misguided fool.

Since he was a rookie, I decided to let him suffer his delusions about who was the guilty party. "I'm headed back to the library." Knowing he'd follow, I headed off.

"You have blood on your arm," he said.

I glanced down and rubbed my arm on the leg of my jeans. Maybe I had busted Norma Rae's lip or something. She shouldn't have scared me so bad with her poor attempt at a joke. "Just Halloween makeup." I continued toward the library and shoved my way through a crowd.

Empty spots on the bookshelves raised my spirits. At this rate, there would be very little to send back to the distributor. I collapsed in a chair, my heart racing like a dog after a rabbit. If I'd busted anything on Norma Rae, she was bound to make a stink about it, regardless that she was the one to start the scuffle.

I leaned my elbow on the table and propped my chin in my hand. Mom bustled from person to person pointing them toward books they might be interested in. Once she caught sight of me, she sat in a chair next to me.

"You look worn out."

"I had a scuffle with Norma Rae in the tunnel. I think I might have bloodied her lip."

"Why?"

"She jumped on my back. I honestly thought she was going to kill me until she laughed and said it was part of her act."

"Was she strong?"

"Yes." I hadn't thought of it until then, but Norma Rae had definitely possessed the strength to choke Mrs. Grimes and she owned the right type of shoes to have left the shoe print outside our store. I needed to head back into the tunnel and find her. But not without an escort.

I eyed Officer Bradford from where he stood by the door. I preferred Bruce. "Can you distract the rookie while I find Bruce?"

Mom nodded. "I'll approach him and faint or something."

"Nothing drastic, just keep him from following me for a minute. The man's like a leech." I pushed to my feet and waited while Mom moved to his side and slipped her arm through his. No one could ever resist her charms when she needed something. Within minutes, she had the poor man moving one of the heavy book crates to the other side of the room. I slipped out the door into the empty school hallway.

Amazing how creepy the halls were without a horde of students rushing through them. With only every other ceiling light illuminated, the hall was cast in shadows and quieter than a tomb. As quietly as possible, not sure who I thought I'd disturb, I made my way down the hall and to the exit door. A sign informed me that an alarm would signal between seven fifteen a.m. and two fifteen p.m. Since it was neither of those times, I should be safe. I pushed the bar and stepped back outside.

That particular door led to a breezeway outside the fence surrounding the football field. So much for a short cut. I increased my pace and headed for the rock wall where hopefully someone could climb up and scout for Bruce.

Sure enough, one of the boys was more than happy to show off his skills. He scampered up like a squirrel and informed me that Bruce was by the cakewalk. "Thanks!" I turned and made my way over. Only two cakes were left. A red velvet with cream cheese frosting and a pan of brownies. I shrugged. I'd been told only store-bought items could be given away and the brownies were clearly made by hand.

"Bruce!" I waved him over.

He glowered and marched toward me. "Where have you been?"

"In the library, why? Don't worry. Your little guard dog has barely left my side."

"He isn't with you now, nor was he with you in the tunnel, was he?"

I opened and closed my mouth like a fish on the shore. "Did I do something wrong?"

He unclipped his handcuffs. "You're under arrest Marsha Steele for assault."

23

I shoved my hands in my pockets in a futile attempt to avoid Bruce's handcuffs. "Who did I assault?" I scanned the crowd for Duane. He made a beeline toward us, still wearing his costume and shoving screaming kids out of his way.

"Norma Rae Jennings. Don't make this any harder than it has to be." Bruce stepped closer. "Don't make me add resisting arrest to your charge."

"Hold on." Freddy, I mean Duane, stepped between me and Bruce. "What's going on?"

Bruce motioned for Duane to step to the side with him. I had half a mind to run while I had the chance. While Bruce spoke too low for me to hear, Duane nodded. He turned, sadness cloaking his eyes.

"It's best you go with him, sweetie." He leaned over and kissed me, giving me a taste of his oily makeup. "I'll be by after we clean all this up."

I nodded and blinked back tears. I held my hands out for Bruce to cuff. "I'm not the guilty party here, and you know it. Norma Rae is the killer." I knew it as if she'd confessed to me herself. I hoped Mom would remember to grab my purse from under the library counter and let Bruce lead me through the gawking crowd to his squad car.

"You have no evidence against Mrs. Jennings," he said, opening the car door. "Watch your head. "But she has plenty against you, a bloody lip for starters and a witness that saw the two of you fighting."

"Did that same witness see her launch herself on my back with a knife in her hand? No? I didn't think so." I sat back and let him close the door. Norma Rae, having failed to kill me in the tunnel, thought having me arrested would protect her identity.

How wrong she was. Duane would bail me out and I'd be after the woman like a duck on a June bug. Arrested! I slammed back against the hard seat. I'd have a criminal record now. Maybe I would write that mystery novel. I had enough material to go on.

I shook my hands, trying to loosen the cuffs that bit into my wrists. As Bruce pulled away from the curb, my gaze locked with Ingrid's. She clamped her lips together and dashed toward the library. Hopefully, she'd let Mom and Lindsey know where I'd gone if Duane hadn't already done so.

A tear escaped and traveled down my cheek to rest in the curve of my lip. I licked the salty wetness away and sniffed.

"Are you crying back there? Seriously, Marsha. Try to see the big picture here, would you?" Bruce shook his head and increased the car's speed.

No way would I give him the satisfaction of conversation. This was the last straw at breaking the camel's back of what tenuous friendship we had. I stared out the window at the night.

All too soon we pulled in back of the station and Bruce opened the back door. With a hand on my elbow, he escorted me inside where I was fingerprinted, the cuffs taken off, and then locked into a cell. At least I wasn't strip-searched. That would have been my final mortification.

A woman sat on a metal bench across from me, her hair hanging in her face. She peered through the dim room at me and smiled. "Company."

I shuddered and turned away.

"Don't be like that. Did you have too much to drink tonight? I did. I'll be out by morning." She moved to sit beside me. The rank odor of beer and body sweat almost overpowered me and it took all the will power I had not to shrink away.

"No, I'm here on assault charges."

"A little bitty thing like you? Who did you attack? A child?" The woman shook her head. "Sometimes the police aren't the brightest things, are they?" She leaned her head against the wall and started snoring.

I moved to the opposite bench and closed my eyes in prayer. I knew God had the situation under control. All I needed to do was trust Him. Hadn't Paul been arrested and counted it all good? I could do the same. At least I wasn't facing persecution.

"Where is my daughter?" Mom's voice rang through the building. "I demand you release her at once, Bruce Barnett. If your mother was alive—"

"She's not getting out until morning, Gertie. It's for her own good."

"Her own good my fanny." The slapping of approaching footprints headed my way. Mom gripped the bars and pressed her face between them. "Are you okay?"

"I'm fine." I rushed to greet her. "He's not allowing you to bail me out?" Tears clogged my throat. I couldn't stay locked up all night.

"No. The cad." Mom handed me a granola bar and a bottle of water. "It's all I could sneak in. Some police officer. He didn't even check my purse."

"Did you grab my purse from the library?"

Her face fell. "It was already gone. I hope Lindsey took it, or Duane, and not some thief." She eyed the woman snoring in the corner. "Is she dangerous?"

I shook my head. "Just drunk. Mom, Norma Rae is the killer. I know it. She tried to stab me in the tunnel. We need evidence."

"I'll find it. I won't sleep tonight until you're free."

After Mom left, I ate the bar and drank half of the water. A big mistake. I squirmed and eyed the toilet in the corner. I'd have to be desperate.

"Marsha?" Duane stood on the other side of the bars with Lindsey.

I cried and ran to him, taking his hands in mine. "Get me out of here."

"We tried. Bruce won't budge." He slipped his face as far through the bars as he could and kissed me.

"He's so mean!" Lindsey crossed her arms and glared. "He said you attacked someone. He doesn't know you very well, does he?"

That's my girl. Forever her mother's supporter. "No, he obviously doesn't. Did you get my purse?"

"No, was I supposed to?"

Great. Add someone stealing my purse, with my Taser, to the growing list of things gone wrong with the day. At least I hadn't taken my gun. Then, Bruce could have arrested me for having a weapon at school. I gasped. "I can't get more charges by having my Taser in the purse, can I? What if a student has it now? Oh, he's going to lock me up forever." I covered my face and slid to the floor.

"Bruce doesn't have your purse," Duane said. "It's probably in the lost and found. I'll check when we leave here."

"Thank you. You two should go now. It's getting late. Bruce said I could get out in the morning. Who's guarding the jail?"

"I am." Bruce joined us. "And yes, visiting hours are over."

After another kiss, Duane and Lindsey left, my daughter giving me a tearful wave on her way.

"I'll be sleeping on a cot in the front room," Bruce said. "Normally, Officer Bradford gets the pleasure, but he has plans tonight. Marsha, I can't post bail until you've seen a judge. You should know that from all the television shows you watch."

Oh, goodie. I didn't know who was worse since they both believed me guilty of something. I turned my back on him and went back to my bench. I lay down and pulled a thin, scratchy blanket over me. I shoved the hard pillow on the floor. If I used that, I'd wake up with lice.

Why was I the only one who knew Norma Rae was the killer? Why hadn't anyone else put the pieces together? Yes, more than one woman wore smooth-soled ballet flats, but the woman attacked me with a knife. That should turn on some light bulbs over people's heads. Except for the important fact that the authorities didn't believe me and I didn't have any witnesses. Since no one was around during our scuffle, where did Norma Rae find someone to vouch for her?

There had to be something I could do to convince them. I mulled over the clues. Motive: Norma Rae needed money in the worst way. Second, I'd witnessed first- hand that she was strong enough to choke or stab someone. Third, she was just plain mean. What woman could treat her daughter the way she treated Ingrid? It was almost as if the woman hated her own daughter. Fourth, the shoes fit. Fifth, the woman knew an awful lot about the crimes. As much or more than Mrs. Willis, in fact.

Mrs. Willis I understood, with her need for research. She'd probably bribed someone into giving her information. But my final answer as to Norma Rae being the killer was the look on Ingrid's face when I mentioned the shoes. That girl knew for a fact who the murderer was and thought to protect her in some misguided attempt at loyalty.

Oh, no! I bolted to a sitting position. What if I wasn't released in the morning? That would set the wedding back even further. I'd be too old to carry another child and I suddenly realized I really did want to have a child with Duane. The tears started fresh.

I plopped back onto the bench, banging my head on the metal surface. Duane might be the most patient person I knew, but even he could give up on me and find someone else. He wouldn't have to try very hard, not with his looks.

I slapped the brick wall. There was no sense in having a pity party. I had to hold onto the fact that Bruce had said I'd be released in the morning. Why then, deny me bail? Was he trying to teach me a lesson about staying out of his investigation? I hadn't been looking for clues when he'd cuffed me. Nothing made sense anymore.

A scuffle sounded from the front room. I sat up and held my breath. When no one came to talk to me or release me, I laid back down. What time was it? Since I didn't have my cell phone or a watch, I could have been locked up for an hour or several. It could be morning for all I knew. I smiled, hoping it was. Then, I'd go before the judge and hopefully be released into Duane's care until they figured out I really wasn't a violent person or a menace to society.

Something rattled from the direction of Bruce's desk. I moved to the bars. "Hello? Who's there?"

When Bruce didn't answer, I scurried back to a corner of the cell. Had Norma Rae come after me even in jail? I sat on the floor, knees bent and arms wrapped around them. Unless she had a gun, I was safe, right? What if she killed Bruce and took his keys. I thought about waking my cell mate and hiding behind her, but thought better of it. I didn't want to be responsible for her getting injured.

"Bruce?" I whispered. My cell mate snuffled in her sleep. A shuffling noise drew closer. I rolled under the bench and hugged the wall. Unless someone turned on the light, they wouldn't be able to see me. Maybe they'd think the snorer was the only occupant.

I held my breath as footsteps paused at the cell then passed. My plan had worked! I grinned and remained as still as possible. The footsteps returned. My heart stopped when they paused in front of the cell for a longer period of time.

A curse word drifted through the darkness. I cringed. I knew that voice. God, help me.

"Marsha," the hoarse whispered words sent shiver down my back. "You have to be here. This is the only cell."

Key's jangled and the cell door squeaked open.

24

"Get out from under there. We don't have much time."

I rolled over and peered into Ingrid's face. "I didn't expect you."

"Mother won't either. Let's go." She reached in and grabbed my arm. "She's only a few minutes behind me."

I crawled from under the bench, and Ingrid handed me my purse. "I grabbed this the moment I spotted Officer Barnett taking you in the squad car. I'm afraid my mother set this up to get you in one easy place."

"Why are you helping me?" I dug in my purse, pleased to see the Taser still there. I shoved it in my bra within easy reach and prayed I wouldn't accidentally zap myself. I'd done that moments after purchasing the thing and had no desire to repeat the experience.

"There's no time. Come on." She rushed out the door.

Bruce's desk was empty, the usually meticulous surface in disarray. Banging came from a door across from us. "Where's Bruce? Shouldn't we stay with him?"

"I locked him in the bathroom. Do you want that fine man to die? Mother will shoot him as easily as you. She's crazy." She whirled to face me, her face as white as chalk. "I've texted Oscar to release him and follow us to the tea room." She sprinted to the parking lot.

I hurried after her. "Why are you doing this?" I asked sliding into the passenger seat of her Sentra.

"I can't let that evil woman kill another person." Ingrid, having been smart enough to leave the car running, pealed rubber onto the highway.

"Is that any way to talk about the woman who raised you?"

We both screamed as Norma Rae's face appeared in the rearview mirror. "You, my dear, are a traitor."

Why hadn't we thought to check the back seat? I reached for the door handle.

"Oh, no, you don't." She clipped me on the back of the head with the pistol she held in her hand. "The next whack will be a bit harder. Now drive, Ingrid."

"Was this a trap to lure me out of the cell?" I put a hand to my head and glared at Ingrid.

"Absolutely not. We're friends. This woman means nothing to me." Ingrid turned the car right.

Norma Rae tsked tsked. "I'm in a difficult position now. Since you're helped my enemy, you'll have to suffer the same fate."

"You'd kill your own daughter?" Nausea burned up my esophagus. I turned to look at her.

"She really isn't my daughter."

I glanced at Ingrid, who shrugged. "It's true. I'm the product of my father's infidelity. Mother either had to raise me or suffer the embarrassment of divorce. It's been a joyless life, you can be sure of that."

"Oh, you poor thing," Norma Rae spat. "How do you think I felt having to raise his bastard child? Do you know the mortification? I would have dropped you at the first hospital if your dear old dad hadn't stipulated in his will that you stay with me. Now, the small amount of money he left me is gone, and I'm still stuck with you."

I was in the middle of a family feud. Ingrid had increased the speed of the car to such a degree that I hooked my seatbelt and held on to the hand strap beside my head. The belt pressed against the Taser, reminding me to look for the first opportunity to use it. I never should have tried to save money by not purchasing the kind that shot out little darts. I so wanted to zap Norma Rae right in her swollen lip. Instead, I relished the knowledge that I was the one who had given her that lip. I'd give her a whole lot more given the chance.

The drive to the tea shop went insanely quick. Ingrid pulled to the front of the shop. I pushed my door open, knocking my purse to the ground.

"I don't think so. Drive around to the back," Norma Rae said. "No funny business."

I slammed my door before she noticed the purse. Of course, anyone in their right mind would look here first. Why weren't we hearing sirens yet? What if Officer Wilson didn't have his phone handy? My spirits sank.

Ingrid followed orders and drove down the alley, slamming the car into park by the shop's back door. "There. Happy." She peered into the rearview mirror.

"Very," Norma Rae said. "Now get out."

She marched us into the store at gunpoint and had us sit at a table. "This is the tricky part." She paced five paces in one direction, then five in the other. "What to do, what to do."

"Why don't you start with telling me why you killed Mrs. Grimes?" Keeping the killer talking worked in the movies, sometimes.

"It's simple, really. I want that infernal map." She dug into her pocket and pulled out the map I'd given Bruce. "Now I have it, and it's time to stop your snooping."

"I seriously doubt there's a treasure." I shook my head. "How did you get that?"

"I had a copy made of Ingrid's key." She grinned, splitting her lip back open. I stared transfixed at a drop of blood beading there. "And if there isn't money to be found where the X marks the spot, then why did dear old Harriet guard it so closely?"

"It's a historical treasure, you old witch." Ingrid crossed her arms. "I've told you a hundred times everyone and their relatives have searched."

"They didn't search hard enough!" Norma Rae turned the gun on her. "I'll do anything not to have to live with you for one more day."

"But Ingrid is getting married," I said. "She'll be living with her new husband, so the two people you murdered were for nothing. Why Stacy?"

"I didn't want a newspaper reporter digging in where she didn't belong. If you could figure out it was me, she definitely would. Stupid girl. When I phoned her and told her to meet me because I had a clue, she couldn't wait to find out what I knew." Norma Rae laughed. "But don't worry. I told her who the murderer was before I killed her."

"You're insane." I'd met crazy people in the last few months, but she was queen of them all.

"Crazy makes me interesting. Now, who should I shoot first?" She moved the gun from Ingrid to me, and then back again. Her hand shook like a person with palsy.

"Do you take meds?" I leaned my elbow on the table. "Did you miss your dosage? Maybe we should take a trip to the pharmacy."

"She hasn't taken them in weeks. Mother suffers from schizophrenia, if you couldn't tell." Ingrid's glare didn't soften despite the promise of death. Good for her. She'd go down fighting.

"Stop telling everyone our business." Norma Rae shifted the gun back to her.

I slipped my hand into my bra and pulled out the Taser. While she was distracted, I slid it under my leg. "I need to use the restroom. Very much." In fact, the need had become painful since I wouldn't use the exposed toilet in the cell.

"You won't need to much longer."

Maybe she cared more for her stepdaughter than she thought. She'd killed Mrs. Grimes and Stacy without a second thought, but now she seemed almost hesitant to shoot either one of us. What was the hold up? Not that I was complaining.

Norma Rae sighed. "This is harder than I thought. After all, I raised one of you and the other has a child. But…there's no help for it." She pulled the trigger, knocking Ingrid out of her chair.

I leaped to my feet, Taser in hand, and rushed her before she could turn the gun in my direction. I pushed the button and watched as she twitched. Another shot went wild before the gun skittered under the counter. Knowing I only had thirty seconds before the effects wore off, I didn't waste time searching for the weapon. Instead, I raced for a door across the room.

It turned out to be a bathroom. I flipped the lock and squeezed between the toilet and the wall, looking at the toilet like it was an unwrapped Christmas present. If I succumbed to my need, I'd be a sitting duck, literally.

"That was not nice!" Norma Rae pounded on the door.

"You shot Ingrid."

"I'm going to shoot you, too." A bullet blasted through the thin door.

Where in the heck was the police? I put my hands over my head and my head between my knees, praying like there wouldn't be another breath. Which, considering the psycho's rage, there might not be. Another bullet blasted the door. One more would make the lock fall to the floor. I needed a plan.

The charge on my Taser showed green. I pushed to my feet and positioned myself against the wall beside the door. Hopefully, she'd continue to shoot the lock and not spray the wall with bullets. The moment she showed her ugly face, I'd zap her again. This time, I would take the gun.

As I'd figured, she shot out the lock. The door slammed open. I grabbed her arm, pulled her into the room, and pressed the Taser against her neck. She dropped like a sack of flour. I grabbed the gun, dropped my pants, and took care of business, all before she could get shakily to her feet. Once I'd finished, I jabbed the gun into her back and shoved the Taser into my pocket. "Your turn." I forced her back to the tables. "Now, you sit."

Ingrid moaned and sat up. "Good thing I thought to borrow a bulletproof vest before freeing you."

I grinned. "Yeah, good thing." I might have gone to lunch with the woman out of a need to dig up information, but at that moment I knew I'd made a true friend. I loved people with guts. "Want me to shoot her?"

"You don't have what it takes," Norma Rae spat.

"Maybe not, but I bet Ingrid does."

Sirens wailed outside. Finally. "Now, you'll be locked up for a very long time and forced to take your meds."

She spit at me. As she sat there, dejected, her hair falling from the bun she always wore, I felt a moment of compassion. She was a sick woman chasing a foolish dream.

Within seconds, Officer Wilson, Bruce, and Duane burst through the front door, shattering the glass. Their eyes widened at the sight of me holding

Norma Rae at gunpoint. Bruce took the gun from me. While Norma Rae moved into her lovers arms, I rushed into Duane's.

He covered my face with kisses before claiming my lips. When we were breathless, he pulled back. "Bruce told me to wait outside, but when I saw your purse on the ground, I needed to see for myself that you were all right. Someone called in that they heard gunshots."

"She shot Ingrid, but Ingrid was wearing a vest, then when I locked myself in the bathroom, she shot the door open. I zapped her with my trusty Taser. Best fifty bucks I ever spent."

"Woman, you make me crazy." He kissed me again, then with his arm around my shoulder, led me to the others.

Bruce cuffed Norma Rae. "Ingrid, it was wrong of you to lock me in the bathroom."

"Are you going to arrest me?"

He shook his head. "You had good intentions, and I'm exhausted from dealing with this case. Duane, I hope your honeymoon is far away from River Valley. I need a break from your bride-to-be."

"Oh, it is." He grinned. "You'll have a ten day break from her."

"I still say your nuts to marry this woman." The soft look in Bruce's eyes belied his words. The man did care about me, and I owed him my life a few times over. "I'm sorry I arrested you, Marsha, but we had our concerns about Norma Rae, and I thought jail was the safest place for you. I was wrong."

I slid from under Duane's arm and planted a

kiss on Bruce's lips. "You'll be next, Officer Barnett. I'm taking it upon myself to find you a wife."

"Heaven help us all." He grabbed Norma Rae's arm and escorted her to his squad car.

I took a deep breath and moved back to the best spot in the world—Duane's embrace.

25

Mom pounded on my bedroom door. "Get up. You'll be late for your own wedding."

I'd been up for hours, unable to sleep, every nerve twanging. The moment I'd waited for my whole life was four hours away. I sat on the edge of the bed and stared at the rag rug at my feet. I'd cared for my first husband, Robert, very much. Still did, even years after he'd died in a car accident.

But my heart had always belonged to his brother Duane. I glanced at the picture of Lindsey on my nightstand. She carried so many traits of the Steele brothers. Duane would be a good father to her.

My wedding dress hung from a hook on the back of the bedroom door. So different from the frilly, lacy gown I'd worn to my first wedding. This one fell to the floor in a cascade of ivory silk. Simple and classy. I moved over to run my hands down the buttery softness. On the dresser sat my veil, long and flowing. The wedding outfit of my dreams.

Since Duane still hadn't told me where our honeymoon was going to be, I'd left my packing to

Mom and followed her strict orders not to peek in the suitcases lined against the wall. I put a hand to my nervous stomach. How long until a baby nestled there? I'd be thirty-six in a few months. It was ridiculous to have a baby at my age. Lindsey was two years from leaving for college, and I'd be starting all over again. The idea frightened and excited me.

"Mom?" Lindsey knocked, then pushed my door open. "Are you ready to head to the lake?"

"More than ready." I draped the wedding gown over my arm and left the veil and beaded heels to Lindsey. "Where's your dress?"

"In the car. We want to get there before Uncle Duane so he doesn't see you. Grandma and I know you're going to want to check out the tables and stuff."

"I sure am." After my fiasco with Norma Rae, no one wanted me to have to lift a finger. I'd already made them all frazzled by adding Ingrid as a last minute bridesmaid, sending Duane rushing to ask Bruce to be a groomsmen.

Yet, it turned out fine and the day was upon us. We stepped outside into a brisk, December day. I'd be married, on my honeymoon, and returned by Christmas. It felt strange not to be involved in the holiday preparations, but I hadn't wanted to move the wedding back any farther.

Leroy grinned and opened the door of a black stretch limousine. "A gift for my ladies."

"You're the sweetest thing." Mom couldn't be luckier to have him as a husband or I to have him as a stepfather. God was good to the Callahan women.

The limo stopped in front of the lake clubhouse. Leroy arrived behind us in his truck and took over carrying in the gowns, shoes, and makeup boxes while we strolled through the reception room and the area inside a glass room where the ceremony would take place. Some might say a December wedding in the Ozarks was too cold, but I loved the chill in the air. A few snowflakes drifted from the slate sky to add a magical feeling to the day. I prayed they'd continue throughout the ceremony and provide a pristine backdrop to the day.

The reception hall was filled with tables draped with starched white tablecloths. In the center of each table, hurricane lamps waited to be lit. Surrounding them were white silk roses, tipped with an iridescent glitter. The whole room sparkled with white lights strung from the ceilings. It really did look like a winter wonderland.

In the glass room, a simple arch adorned with the same lights and flowers of the reception hall waited for me and Duane. Tears pricked my eyes. It was so beautiful in its simplicity.

"It's time to get dressed." Mom slipped her arm in mine. "It's going to be the most beautiful wedding of the year."

I agreed, but then we might both be biased. We headed for a room set aside for the bride. The photographer, a woman from church, waited with a big grin. "I like to take candid shots of the wedding party getting ready," she said. "Then, I'll take all the pictures of the bride with her girls before meeting up with the guys."

Ingrid rushed into the room. "Sorry I'm late. I

stopped by to see Mother."

I raised my eyebrows.

"I know, I know, but she's the only mother I've ever known, even if she is fruitier than a can of Del Monte." Ingrid slipped out of the skirt and blouse she wore and into the bridesmaid gown. The rose color brightened her complexion.

"The makeup lady is here to do all of our makeup," I told her. "I hope you don't mind."

"I've never worn makeup before."

"You'll be gorgeous." I sat at a vanity and turned myself over to the woman's ministrations. There was nothing more soothing than someone doing your hair and makeup. No wonder it had become so popular for brides to hire someone. It helped relax them before the vows.

"The men are here." Lindsey rushed into the room and slammed the door. "Uncle Duane looks fine!"

The rest of us giggled. She narrowed her eyes. "What? He does. Someday, I want to marry a man just like him."

I patted her hand. "He's a fine example to hold your future husband up to. A godly man who puts the woman he loves first and doesn't hold her back when she feels strongly about pursuing something." Although Duane was most often less than thrilled about my latest crime solving spree, he'd chosen to support me rather than stifle. I loved him for it.

An hour later, I stood behind two double doors, my arm linked with Leroy's. His eyes glistened with tears. "Thank you for allowing me this honor."

I stood on tip toe and planted a kiss on his ruddy

cheek. "The pleasure is all mine."

The strains of the wedding march reached us and the doors opened. First, a lovely, very feminine looking stranger named Ingrid, small stepped down the aisle, followed by Lindsey. Then the music increased in volume. I took a shaky breath and my first step down the aisle toward my handsome man.

He was splendid in a dark tuxedo. His eyes shimmered and never left my face as Leroy slipped my hand into his. I heard very little of the ceremony, getting a nudge in the back from my daughter when it was time to repeat the vows the pastor said. I giggled and repeated them.

"I now pronounce you man and wife. You may kiss your bride."

No sweeter words ever reached my ears. Duane dipped me back and planted a heavy kiss on my lips, raising me back up to hoots and yells from most of his football team. He nuzzled my ear. "How does an Alaskan cruise sound for a honeymoon?"

"I'd go to the barren dessert of Africa as long as I went with you." I grinned. "But the cruise sounds much more wonderful."

He straightened me and we turned to face our family and friends for the first time as husband and wife.

The End

Be sure to check out the first two books in the River Valley mystery series:
Book One: Deadly Neighbors
Book Two: Advance Notice

Also check out another series by Cynthia Hickey, The Summer Meadows Series
Book One: Fudge-Laced Felonies
Book Two: Candy-Coated Secrets
Book Three: Chocolate-Covered Crime
Book Four: Maui Macadamia Madness

To see her books in other genres…visit her website at www.cynthiahickey.com

ABOUT THE AUTHOR

www.cynthiahickey.com

Cynthia Hickey is a multi-published and best-selling author of cozy mysteries and romantic suspense. She has taught writing at many conferences and small writing retreats. She and her husband run the publishing press, Winged Publications. They live in Arizona and Arkansas, becoming snowbirds with three dogs. They have ten grandchildren who keep them busy and tell everyone they know that "Nana is a writer."

www.ingramcontent.com/pod-product-compliance
Lightning Source LLC
LaVergne TN
LVHW011816060526
838200LV00053B/3806